The Meanest Teacher

The
Meanest Teacher

JONI EARECKSON TADA
STEVE JENSEN

CROSSWAY BOOKS • WHEATON, ILLINOIS
A DIVISION OF GOOD NEWS PUBLISHERS

The Meanest Teacher
Copyright © 2001 by Joni Eareckson Tada and Steve Jensen
Published by Crossway Books
        a division of Good News Publishers
        1300 Crescent Street
        Wheaton, Illinois 60187

Previously published as *Darcy and the Meanest Teacher in the World*
by Chariot Books, an imprint of David C. Cook Publishing Co., in 1993.

Cover design: Cindy Kiple
Cover illustration: Matthew Archambault
First printing 2001
Printed in the United States of America

Library of Congress Cataloging-in-Publication Data
Tada, Joni Eareckson.
   [Darcy and the meanest teacher in the world]
   The meanest teacher / Joni Eareckson Tada and Steve Jensen.
     p. cm. — (Darcy and Friends ; 3)
   Previously published as: Darcy and the meanest teacher in the world.
   Summary: Twelve-year-old Darcy, trying to project a "normal" image
in junior high school despite her wheelchir, runs for office with the
promise of exposing cruel and unfair teachers in the school, until prayer
and her friends reveal to her that every situation has two sides.
   ISBN 1-58134-256-X (tpb : alk. paper)
   [1. Wheelchairs—Fiction. 2. Physically handicapped—Fiction.
3. Schools—Fiction. 4. Christian life—Fiction.] I. Jensen, Steve.
II. Title.
PZ7.T116 Md 2001
[Fic]—dc21   2001000585
                                                           CIP

15	14	13	12	11	10	09	08	07	06	05	04	03	02	01
15	14	13	12	11	10	9	8	7	6	5	4	3	2	1

To Alex, Jani, and Ricky—
Three friends of Jesus with bright smiles and warm hugs

One

"He-e-e-lp!"

I strained my ears for the sound of someone galloping down the dirt path on a white horse to rescue me, but all I heard was my own screechy echo. I glanced over my shoulder at the mud below me—thick, yucky goo that smelled suspiciously of horse manure. My horse Poncho shifted his weight, and I tightened my hands around the saddle horn.

"Somebody, he-e-e-lp!"

I had to giggle. I sounded exactly like Sylvia Farbman the day she crawled into her locker on a dare, only to have someone slam the door shut. But this was no time to be thinking about Sylvia Farbman. I was in real trouble. If only I hadn't reached for that stupid bird's nest in the tree above me, I wouldn't be stuck over this muddy grand canyon.

Fortunately Poncho seemed content to stay where there was plenty of tall grass. I had tied him to a bush before I reached for the nest, so he would stay put. But now, hanging halfway between horse and mud, I wished I hadn't tied him up. It would be great if Poncho could break loose and head back home with me holding on, the way it happens in the movies when a cowboy's been wounded. "PONCHO A HERO!" the headlines would blare. "GIRL SAVED BY TRICK HORSE!" But this wasn't the movies.

I yelled one more time, "Hey, out there! I need help!"

More echoes. I sighed and tried climbing back into the saddle, but with no help from my paralyzed legs, my arms were not strong enough. I tried to loosen the reins. Nothing worked. I was stuck, and I'd just have to hold on until somebody came down the path. My biceps may be perfect for pushing a wheelchair, but at the moment they were aching.

I felt very alone and scared.

❊ ❊ ❊

This whole mess began when my friend Mandy Ellis and I decided to go horseback riding in Willowbrook Park. We grew up in this town, and we've played together in this park since kindergarten. Now that we're in seventh grade, Mandy and I have graduated from My Little Ponies in the sandbox to real horses at the park stable.

We rent Poncho and Cactus whenever we save up enough money—ten dollars for the first hour, fifteen for two hours. We always try to save up for long rides. Willowbrook Park has a pond, nature trails, and beautiful trees that turn all colors this time of year. Mandy and I like to talk and giggle and think when we go riding. Riding horses is a great way to escape and think.

Now that Mandy and I are in seventh grade, thinking seems more important than ever. I think about things I never thought about before. For example, when I went to Willowbrook Elementary, I never used to think about whether my jeans looked okay. Or why does my hair have to be so straight when everyone else in my family has nice hair? And why do my freckles look like they're exploding all over my face?

It's not so much that things were perfect in elementary school. I've always had freckles and straight hair and clothes that didn't fit right. But now I spend what seems like hours in front of the mirror trying to fix whatever is wrong with me.

Mom says I'm just growing up and learning about myself. She uses fancy words such as *self-esteem* and *self-concept.* "I remember feeling the same way you do, Darcy," she says. Sure. It's hard to imagine Mom being anything other than Mom. I can't believe she ever worried about who her friends were or how to avoid falling into a mud pit while dangling from a horse.

Anyway Mandy and I had been riding along, thinking about life when she asked me a question: "Are you daydreaming about that boy in English class, Darcy?"

I knew she was teasing, but I answered, "Hah! Who cares about boys? They're so gross. Except, of course, for Chip. He's normal. I wish all the boys at Jordan were like him. School wouldn't be so hard."

"That's for sure. School hasn't been in session two weeks, but already seventh grade is tough. All those thick textbooks and the different classrooms and the crowded hallways. And I hate taking showers after phys. ed.," Mandy groaned.

"The lunchroom is a zoo," I commented.

"And they never warned us about all that homework," she put in.

"And the other kids dress nicer and seem smarter."

"And faster," added Mandy. "I used to be the fastest girl at Willowbrook Elementary, but now I feel like a hippo."

Mandy is no hippo. Mandy is fast. Before the auto

accident that put me in a wheelchair, she and I were the fastest kids in second grade. Her pigtails could be seen bouncing in the wind by every jealous boy who could not keep up. But everything was different now, and we were just going to have to face it: Jordan Junior High would be the biggest test of our twelve-year-old lives. Just knowing Mandy felt the same way I did eased some of the pressure. We would be faithful, stand-up-for-each-other friends. Changes or no changes. Hippos forever! I laughed as I imagined Mandy and me as hippos wearing shorts and Reeboks. Then she interrupted my private joke: "I think junior high is going to be where we find out who our true friends are."

Who our true friends are? The thought shook me hard. Suddenly the picture of Mandy, the high-jumping hippo, disappeared. I had to know what she meant. "You know who your true friends are," I said, a little defensively. "Chip and April and me. Nothing's going to change that." I tried to hide the worry in my words.

"Darcy, you said it yourself. School is hard. So many things are different. The pressure is bound to make changes, even with friends."

I could tell Mandy didn't want to get me upset or hurt my feelings. I could always trust her to tell me the truth and to stick by me. But when I thought about all the other kids at our new school, especially the cool group of kids in Mandy's homeroom, I couldn't help but feel a little worried.

That's when I started some serious daydreaming and let Poncho amble at his own pace. We fell further behind Mandy and Cactus on the path. She saw an open stretch and gave Cactus a kick, calling out, "Come on, hippo. I'll race ya!"

But I was still worrying about friends, and I didn't want to run. "I'll meet you at the stable!" I yelled.

What kind of friend was she anyway, telling me this was the year that we would find out who our true-blue buddies were? Nothing was going to come between my friends and me!

And that's when it happened. As I turned the bend before the open stretch, I saw a bright red maple tree out of the corner of my eye. One of the branches hung low and close to the trail, and hanging from the branch was a bird's nest. It was as if someone had hung a sign on it that said, "This nest is here for the taking by any junior high student wanting to get extra credit in biology class."

I reined Poncho off the trail a few yards underneath the branch and reached for the nest, but it was just a couple of inches too high. Throwing the reins over a small bush to keep Poncho from moving, I pushed with my left hand in order to lift off the saddle a bit. I reached for the nest with my right hand and—

Yikes! I lost my balance, slipped, and slid halfway down the side of the saddle. My one leg was nearly through the stirrup, just enough to stop me from falling into the mud below. So there I stayed, hanging off the side of my horse, clinging to the horn for dear life. The nest was still swaying in the breeze, clinging to the branch. If it weren't for the stirrup and the saddle horn, I would have been swimming with the muddy tadpoles.

But I couldn't hold on forever. Even worse, my paralyzed legs wouldn't help me in a fall. If I let go, I could break a leg—or two.

I took one more deep breath. "He-e-e-e-e-l-p!"

Mandy was too far ahead to know I was in trouble. My mind raced.

Oh, why did I ever get into this mess?! I wish I had never reached up for that branch. I wish I had never come horseback riding today. I wish I had never learned to ride. And I just bought this sweater yesterday, and you're my best friend, Mandy Ellis, and I'll never do this again, and help me, Lord . . .

My sweaty, weak hands lost their grip. Gravity took over.

Two

It only happens in the movies.

Someone, usually the dumb heroine, is about to get run over by a bulldozer or fall off a cliff. Then along comes the hero at the last minute to save the day. Everyone falls in love and lives happily ever after. End of story.

As I said, this was no movie. However, just as my fingers lost their grip, I felt someone grab the back of my belt. I rose into the air and landed—plop!—on Poncho's saddle. Shocked and relieved, I turned to see a guy standing almost as tall as his horse and smiling at me. He wore dirty jeans, a checkered shirt, and a cowboy hat.

"Going for a ride, young lady?" he asked.

"Uh, yeah . . . trying to," I said weakly. "I was

reaching for that nest up there when I slipped. I would have gotten back in the saddle, but my legs are para- lyzed, and I can't—"

"I get the picture, miss. Were you riding alone?"

"I was riding with my friend, but she went on ahead, and I started daydreaming and lost track of her."

"It's a good thing I came along when I did then. I'm Chuck. I just started working at the stable weekends while I go to college. What's your name?"

"I'm Darcy. Darcy DeAngelis," I said as I adjusted myself in the saddle. I was looking down, rubbing my aching arms, when I saw how high the mud was around his boots. Even the bottoms of his jeans were dirty.

"Oh no! I'm really sorry. Look what happened to your nice boots."

"Don't worry about that. They've been through worse piles of horse manure." Chuck made a small bow. "Besides, I wouldn't be much of a gentleman if I let a pretty damsel in distress ruin her day because I cared more about a pair of boots."

Damsel in distress. You would have had to be there to know why my face got red and why I suddenly thought Chuck, a college-aged, muddy stable hand, was a handsome prince.

"Well, I . . . uh . . . better get back to the stable. My friend will be waiting for me," I said.

"I'll ride back with you. Let me tighten your saddle a bit. It got loose while you were hanging on it."

While Chuck stepped through the mud to tighten the cinch, I looked up and saw the nest still perched in the tree. As eager as I had been to have it just a few minutes ago, the idea now seemed silly, childish. I hoped the "gentleman cowboy" wouldn't remember that I was after it.

Chuck finished cinching up my saddle and got on his horse. "All set?" he asked.

"Sure. Let's go."

Chuck led the way. As we got back on the trail, he stopped. "Hey, we almost forgot. You wanted that nest. Let me go get it."

And before I could stop him, he had reined his horse toward the tree and given him a kick.

"No, that's okay," I called out as I watched his hand pluck the nest off the branch. My feeble protest didn't stop him. He wedged the nest between my lap and the saddle horn and then headed for the stable. I slapped Poncho with my reins and followed at a trot.

When we arrived, Mandy was waiting with her hands on her hips and an impatient look on her face.

"Where were you?" she fumed.

"Off being rescued," I said, still feeling like a damsel in distress. "This is Chuck. He works here on weekends now that he's started college."

I said the word *college* with a little more empha-
sis than necessary, hoping to see a little envy in Mandy's
face. I wasn't disappointed. I went on to tell the story
in a matter-of-fact way, as if it were no big deal to get
stranded over a pile of mud.

We made our way to the stable ramp where I got
off the horse and into my wheelchair.

"I don't suppose you can pop wheelies in that
chair?" Chuck asked admiringly.

"Not yet, but I'm working on it. I'll give you a
demonstration sometime. I can go so fast in it you'd
probably have a hard time keeping up," I teased, feeling
a little cocky.

Mandy looked at me in surprise. I certainly wasn't
sounding like a twelve-year-old!

Chuck headed toward the stable. "You're on, kid.
But right now I've got to get back to unloading the feed
truck. See you two around." He waved good-bye with
his hat.

"See ya," I responded.

"That's the last time I leave you daydreaming on
the horse trail by yourself, Darcy!" Mandy declared. We
stifled our giggles, looking back to see if we could still
spy on Chuck. He was in the stable and out of sight,
so we headed out of the park, letting our laughter fill
the air.

※ ※ ※

The rest of the weekend was fairly routine. My older sister Monica had a few of her girlfriends over to do their nails and make hot fudge sundaes. Mom and Dad threw a barbecue for Josh's Cub Scout den—he and a few others were graduating into Boy Scouts. Our newest family member, a golden retriever named EJ, got a bath.

The only thing out of the ordinary was my rubbing sticky liniment into my sore arms all day. And on Sunday morning Monica had to push me up the church ramp and down the center aisle all the way to the front pew. That made me feel a little handicapped, but my hands were all callused, and my arms ached from my adventure. I had always thought I was pretty strong, but hanging from the horse had stretched muscles I didn't know I had.

By Monday the pain wasn't as great, but I was ticked off. Everything was going wrong. My shirt gave me a rash around my neck and pulled out of my jeans whenever I leaned forward. I had a pimple on my chin (probably from Saturday's hot fudge sundae). The old Ninja Turtle stickers I had glued onto the sides of my wheelchair back in elementary school were still there. I had planned to scrape them off over the weekend, but my arms had been too sore. And my jeans looked dumb. They were all stretched out so they bunched up around my middle in a big bubble. I tried to cover it up with the book bag.

When the bell for first period rang, I left home-room and headed for social sciences. I was glad that all we had to do was listen to the first row of kids read their reports on the drug wars in South America. I kept thinking of Mom's lectures about "just say no" and the anti-drug T-shirt stuffed in the back of my bottom dresser drawer. I don't know why the teacher made such a big deal about drugs. Most of the kids I knew thought drugs were stupid. But the reports were inter-esting enough to get my thoughts off my looks, at least for first period.

Second period was another story. It was literature class, and we were studying Greek mythology. I had written a report about Medusa, the lady with the snakes in her hair, and I was to give it in front of the class that morning.

Great. I have to give a report in front of the class with a war zone for a chin and jeans that belong in the Goodwill bag and Ninja Turtle stickers on my chair.

When the bell rang, I wheeled to the opposite end of the building to the elevator. My classroom was on the sec-ond floor. Battling through the hallway in a wheelchair with 800 junior high students is no easy trick. "Excuse me. . . . I'm sorry. . . . Watch your toes. . . . Sorry. . . . Wheelchair coming through," I said with a forced smile. I wished Chip or Mandy were around to run block.

It took me forever to get to the elevator. I pushed the button and waited, looking at my watch. The light was lit, but I didn't hear any noise of motors or cables through the elevator door. As I pushed the button for the third time, I heard the bell ring for the start of second period.

"Oh, great. What a day. I did my devotions today, Lord! Why is this happening?" I said out loud.

I had been told that if I couldn't get around the building for some reason, I could go to the school office and find someone to help me. So I took off as fast as I could down the hall. As I turned the corner, I almost ran over Mr. Williams, the janitor. I grabbed my hand rims and slid to a halt, missing his shins by less than an inch. I stopped in time, but the book bag on my lap flew through the air and hit his knees.

"Oh, hi, Mr. Williams. I'm sorry." I was out of breath, talking rapidly between gulps of air. "The elevator's stuck, and I'm late for class, and I have to give a report."

"I'm on my way, young lady. The elevator man was here this morning and told me this might happen. I can fix it in a jiffy."

Mr. Williams pushed me down the hall to the elevator. He must have sensed I was upset because he started philosophizing.

"Yep. I remember being in seventh grade. Nothing went right. Everything I said or did made trouble— felt like a porcupine in a balloon factory."

I was in no mood for a counseling session. I was concentrating on Medusa's snake-filled hair. Somehow snakes and porcupines didn't mix well.

We arrived at the elevator where Mr. Williams opened a panel and flipped a switch. The motor started up, and soon the elevator doors opened, and we entered.

"I'll ride up with ya to be sure it don't get stuck," said Mr. Williams. "Hee, hee, wouldn't that make your day—being stuck in an elevator by yourself!"

I smiled politely as the elevator stopped at the second floor. The doors opened, and I sped out and down the hall, calling out thanks as I left Mr. Williams in the dust. I heard him yell an offer to take me to class and explain things to my teacher.

"That's okay. I'm sure Mr. Dempsey won't mind," I called back.

Actually I wasn't sure Mr. Dempsey wouldn't mind. He seemed kind of strict, but I hoped he would understand. I came in the back door of the classroom in order to attract less attention. Fat chance.

Mr. Dempsey stopped in the middle of his sentence. "Welcome to class, Miss DeAngelis. It's so good of you to join us," he said sarcastically.

"The elevator wasn't working, and I had to wait for Mr. Williams to come and fix it," I said.

There must have been something threatening about machines to Mr. Dempsey. The word *elevator* stopped him in his tracks.

"I see. Well, I was just explaining to the class that all of you will be writing an assignment during class after you give us your report on Agamemnon."

"Agamemnon?" I blurted out before I could think. "I did my report on Medusa!"

"No, Darcy. That's Jose's report. You were to present Agamemnon today," said Mr. Dempsey. "Listen carefully next time. I know that being handicapped is hard. If you need help reviewing assignments, perhaps one of your friends can assist you. And if we moved you to the front of the class, you could hear and see a little better. Don't you agree?"

I couldn't answer. I was fuming. How dare this person think I was deaf and blind and stupid! *Of all the insensitive, idiotic . . . Who does he . . . I'm so embarrassed I could . . .* My face was red-hot, and my eyes were filling with tears. I knew everyone was looking at me.

"Please prepare your report on Agamemnon for

tomorrow. We might have time to listen to both you and Jose then." Mr. Dempsey dropped the subject and went on to explain the next class assignment.

We were to think about a true experience we had had and write about it as if we were Sophocles or Homer or one of those other writers of Greek mythology. We were to explain the event as if the Greek gods were somehow involved in making the event happen.

There were the usual groans from the class until Mr. Dempsey cut everyone off with, "You'll enjoy it more than you think. Now you'll be graded on your creativity as well as your writing. Follow all the rules of grammar and check your spelling. I don't expect you to finish in class today, but hand it in at the end of class so I can see your progress."

There were questions about how long the paper had to be and if we had to write with pen or pencil. Someone asked if we could make up Greek gods of our own. That idea got shot down. As the questions continued, I started writing. A silent hour of thinking and writing would be just fine with me. I chose my topic in a flash.

I wrote about my experience with the horse over the weekend. I envisioned a Greek god moving the branch out of the way and another one sending a thunderstorm to create the mud. I made Chuck the stable hand into Hercules! I had actually finished the entire story when the bell rang. As the kids tore out the pages to hand in, I had one last idea, not about the event but about the idea of Greek gods. I wrote the following:

"Some of the Greek myths are interesting, but I know they were invented by people to explain things. Because I believe in God who made me and everything in the world, I don't have to worry about some jealous or lazy Greek god deciding what my fate will be. God knew what would happen this weekend, and He took care of me and kept me from breaking my legs."

Maybe devotions this morning had a purpose all along, I thought to myself. I wanted to write more, but I ran out of time. As I handed it in, I wondered what Mr. Dempsey would think.

Maybe be doesn't believe in God, I worried. *Maybe he'll think I wrote that stuff just to show that I'm not stupid or that I've got God on my side. Worse yet, maybe he'll think I'm putting him down for picking on me earlier! Or . . . oh no, maybe he'll think I'm a spiritual show-off.*

It was too late to change my mind. The kid in the front row had collected all the papers and stacked them on Mr. Dempsey's desk. Mr. Dempsey put his hands around the papers and placed them in his briefcase. I sighed, loaded up my things, and headed for the next class.

Three

"Over here, Darcy!" I heard Mandy yell as I entered the cafeteria at lunch time. She had gotten in line and was saving me a place. "Grilled cheese sandwiches and tomato soup," she groaned as I approached.

I corrected her. "You mean red paint and grease pucks."

That got a big laugh out of the others in line. The food wasn't really that bad, but complaining about it was the thing to do. After the laughter and the glow of feeling smart passed away, I fell in line in front of Mandy and quietly confessed, "I sure wasn't in a joking mood this morning. I'm still sore from our ride on Saturday, and my face feels like it's turning into one big zit. Then the elevator got stuck and made me late for literature, and I was so embarrassed by Mr. Dempsey. He made me feel really dumb."

"Maybe you are, Darcy," Mandy kidded.

I scowled at her, which made her laugh harder.

"The problem with you, Darcy DeAngelis, is that you think too much about how you feel. Loosen up, will ya? Besides, you don't know the true meaning of embarrassment. You wouldn't believe what happened to me in French class. Michael Frederick wrote something really stupid about me in a note he passed to Chip. The teacher caught the note and made Chip read it out loud. I could have died right there."

Her story did sound worse than mine.

"Well? What did the note say?" I didn't get a chance to hear her answer.

Crash!

While I was looking at Mandy, my tray had pushed the tray of the kid in front of me over the end of the rail—like a train car over the edge of a cliff. Chocolate pudding dripped from the wall and peach slices splattered across the floor, swimming in a syrup of peach juice and tomato soup.

"Way to go, Angle Nose!" the kid yelled. "Where'd you learn a stupid trick like that?"

Somehow this big excuse for an eighth grader had picked up on my last name and promptly let the entire junior high know who was at fault. Everyone stared at me to see what would happen, but not too many laughed out loud. After all, who wants to laugh at a crip? Poor crippled people can't help making dumb mistakes, right?

While I sat there, staring at the mess, Mandy quickly grabbed hold of my chair. "C'mon, Darcy, grab your tray. Let's go sit down—fast!"

We went around the tomato soup, but couldn't avoid the sliced peaches. My wheels smashed a couple of pieces and got sticky syrup all over my tires. Even my hands got wet from the goo as I wheeled myself through the cafeteria. I glanced behind me. I had left tracks all the way from the cash register through the door to the courtyard and our table outside under the tree.

"Mandy, I can't stand it." I started to cry. "Nothing is going right. I hate it here. I don't want to stay in school."

"Darcy, you gotta hang in there. What happened to your strong, don't-give-up-without-a-fight chin?" She gave me an extra napkin so I could wipe my hands.

"It's got a zit on it, that's what!" I laughed as I wiped my hands and then my eyes. "Don't try to cheer me up. You don't know what it's like. I don't care if Michael Frederick embarrassed you, it's not the same.

You try sitting in this—this cage for a while and see how you feel."

I had done it again. A couple of years ago I had promised Mandy I wouldn't use my wheelchair as a way of protecting my feelings. But this time I was hurting so badly I just couldn't help it.

Mandy didn't say anything. She looked at the ground and picked at her sandwich. I didn't feel like eating either. We both appreciated the chance to be silent.

The sun felt good as the cool breeze blew through the courtyard. I looked at the kids playing basketball, then at the windows of the cafeteria, the roof, and then the sky. There was no answer written in the clouds, but looking around helped me to think more clearly.

I broke the silence. "Something has to happen, Mandy. I've got to find a way to feel a part of things. I did it at Willowbrook Elementary, and I can do it here."

"You mean find a way to feel . . . normal?" Mandy asked in a "we've-been-over-this-before" tone of voice.

"Oh, don't start, Mandy. I've heard that speech. 'I'm just like anybody else.' But how do the other kids know that? All they see is someone in a wheelchair, coming late to class, doing the wrong assignment, bumping people's lunch off the counter, making the peaches skate across the floor." I couldn't help smiling.

"That cafeteria lady—she looked like a horror movie with tomato soup on her face!" Mandy smirked.

We rehearsed the disaster, laughing uncontrollably. Each comment made the event even more disastrous and comical. When our fits of laughter quieted down, I finally said, "I know I'm normal, Mandy. You know I'm normal. Chip and April know. It just hurts not to be able to show everybody else I am."

Mandy was about to reply when the loudspeaker squeaked. "Good afternoon," said the voice of the vice principal. "Here are the announcements for the day. There will be cheerleading tryouts tomorrow, Tuesday afternoon, in the gym. All those interested should be there by 3:15."

"April is a shoo-in for cheerleading," I said.

April was a natural at that kind of thing. She was pretty, with shiny red hair. She could do flips and jumps, and she had a voice that could stop a train.

"The Journalism Club will meet Tuesday at 3:15 in Room 304. The Chess Club will meet Thursday at 3:15 in Room 111. Anyone interested in either of those clubs is encouraged to attend."

I was about to make another comment about April's cheerleading potential when the vice principal said something that caught my ear: "Student government elections are two weeks away. Those interested in running for office must attend a pre-election meeting in the assembly hall this afternoon. This meeting is for both new candidates and those running for reelection."

"That's it!" I said to Mandy.

"That's what?"

"I'll run for student government."

"You can't be serious. What would you run for?"

"President. What else?"

"But do you know . . . I mean . . . do you have a reason to run, Darcy? You can't just say, 'I want to be president.' You have to have a platform—you know, a view on school matters. Have you thought about that?"

Mandy always thought of questions I couldn't answer.

"I don't know yet, but I'll figure that out later. 'Darcy for president.' Doesn't that sound great? Hey, with my brain and your management, I'm a shoo-in!"

"Me—your manager?" she protested. "What makes you think I could—" My puppy-dog eyes stopped Mandy cold. "Oh, all right. But you'd better know what you're getting into."

"No sweat, kiddo. This'll be great," I assured her. "Hey, the lunchroom disaster was just a brilliant campaign strategy. It's called exposure. Now everyone knows my name!"

"Right. Angle Nose. Vote for Angle Nose,"

announced Mandy with a pretend megaphone to an imaginary crowd. "She's got the angle on Jordan Junior High!"

We both laughed as we returned to the cafeteria to put our trays away. As we walked down the hall, Mandy finally got to tell me her story about Michael Frederick's note.

"The note said I was cute, and Chip should ask me to the football game on Saturday," Mandy concluded.

Boy, she was right. She won the embarrassment award for the day. I felt bad for Chip too. He was a super friend to both Mandy and me, and we could imagine how he felt. I was about to ask if she thought Chip would actually ask her when I heard someone call my name.

It was Mr. Dempsey. I felt myself tighten up as he approached. "There you are, Darcy. Would you try to get to class a minute or two early tomorrow? I want to talk to you about the story you wrote in class today." He sounded serious.

"Okay, Mr. Dempsey. I'll do my best."

He turned and walked back down the nearly empty hallway.

I waited until he was out of sight and then said to Mandy, "This is a royal disaster. I have never, ever been in trouble with a teacher in my entire life!" I looked at her in disbelief. "What's next? Will I come to school with two different shoes on?"

Mandy shook her head with a soft smile and put her arm around me. "Look, it's not often I suggest this right in the middle of school," she said as she glanced around, "but let's pray, okay?"

"Right here in the hallway?" I protested. Even though no one was around, I didn't really feel like praying, especially in a hallway. At any time a kid could come out of one of the rooms.

"There's a study room right down the hall," she said. "It'll be quiet in there."

I rolled my eyes, but Mandy had done this to me before. And if I protested too much, she would think I wasn't very spiritual—which at the moment was true.

Mandy and I had grown up together in our church's Sunday school, and we shared some really special memories from camp and stuff. We enjoyed talking about things like heaven and whether or not the devil made us tell white lies or if it was just us doing it. For Mandy and me, this was ordinary conversation for sleepovers or rainy Saturday afternoons in our rooms.

But at that moment, I didn't want to talk about Jesus or to Jesus. My mind was wanting to get busy with plans for my campaign. I thought being busy would help me forget my awful day. And every minute that I worked on my election would bring me closer to having the other kids see the real me. After all, I was sure that God was the one who had given me the great idea about running for president.

But I followed Mandy into the small study room down the hall from the cafeteria and parked just to the left of the door.

Mandy took a deep breath and prayed, "Dear Lord, Darcy is really hurting right now. It's been a bad morning for her. You know that, and You know how she feels. So I pray that she would have a good afternoon and that she'll know that You are with her the whole way. Help her to make the right decision about running for president. And help her as she talks with Mr. Dempsey tomorrow." She waited a second or two and then added, "Amen."

We were silent for a moment after Mandy ended her prayer. I still didn't feel like praying, but I was too ashamed not to. I mumbled, "Lord, thank You for, uh, loving me. Please be with me today and help me not to feel so out of it." I stopped to see if anything else would come to mind and then added, "Help me as I make plans for the election. In Jesus' name. Amen."

Mandy and I looked at each other for a moment, and then she said, "It's going to be all right, Darcy. You'll see. You just have to trust God for everything and let Him do it."

Mandy turned my wheelchair around and gave me a push out into the hallway. I turned left, and she turned right, saying, "The bell is going to ring in two minutes. You'd better get started for the elevator."

✳ ✳ ✳

I wheeled into the assembly hall and pulled up next to a table in the middle of the room. I was one of the first ones there and didn't see anyone I knew. Then I heard April's voice.

"Darcy! I can't believe it. You're running for election too? What are you going to run for? Secretary? I heard being secretary isn't that bad. You have to write a lot, and you end up doing all the invitations for parties and stuff, but you're good at that."

April was a nonstop talker, and as she plopped her books down next to me, she barely took a breath before she continued. "Did you know I'm running for treasurer? I've got this neat idea for selling pizza at football games. See, we give each person in our class a free piece of pizza and then have them go out in the stands. Then when the other people in the stands smell it and see it, they'll come back to buy some at the booth. Won't that be great?"

I smiled and said, "Sounds terrific. In fact, if I win the election for president, it'll be the first thing you'll do as treasurer."

"President? You're going to run for president?" April's voice was a little too loud and not too encouraging.

"Yes, I am," I said. If I were going to be president, I couldn't back down just because someone challenged me.

"Well, it's your choice, Darcy. Good luck." April went to the front of the room.

A tall Oriental girl with long black hair appeared and sat down next to me.

"Hi. My name is Kendra Takahashi. You're Darcy, aren't you?"

It was the strangest last name I'd ever heard, but I wasn't going to ask her to repeat it. "Yeah, I'm Darcy. How did you know?"

"Chip told me about you. He said you were friends and went to Willowbrook Elementary together. Chip and I work on the school paper. We're both reporters."

Chip had only been working on the school paper a week, but Kendra made it sound like they were best buddies. Hmmm. He had told me that working on the paper was great. Maybe Kendra was the reason.

Not Chip, I thought to myself. *He's still into sports,*

not girls. Besides, this girl's an eighth grader. He's certainly not into . . . older women.

At least I hoped not. I tried to remember the last time we had really talked the way we used to. At Willowbrook Chip, Mandy, and I were the leaders. And we used to hang out after class and talk about everything from sports to comics to Jesus. But now there were so many other things to occupy our time. Maybe Chip had changed.

". . . I said, 'What are you going to run for?'" Kendra asked.

"Oh, I'm sorry. I think I'm going to run for president," I said, a little embarrassed at being caught daydreaming during a conversation.

Kendra swung her hair over her shoulder. "Really? You've got guts. Not many seventh graders do that. They mostly run for student representative or vice president."

"I considered it," I said, "but I think I can do this."

"You know what? I bet you can," Kendra replied as the faculty adviser stepped into the room. She whispered, "A bunch of us are going over to the roller rink this afternoon. Do you want to come?"

"Sure. They won't let me on the floor, but I can watch," I whispered back.

Wow, an eighth grader asking me to do stuff! I

smiled, settled into my chair, and felt a surge of confidence as the meeting got started. The adviser told us all the details about getting elected. After he talked about the responsibilities of each office, I knew I had made the right decision.

And meeting Kendra was an extra answer to prayer. I thought back on that prayer time with Mandy after lunch, and I also thought back to Saturday when we had gone horseback riding. Mandy had said we'd learn who our real friends were going to be.

I looked at Kendra, who was leaning on her elbow, twisting a strand of her long black hair. *Maybe she's going to be a really good friend,* I thought. *She's the only one, so far, who seems to believe I can do a good job of running for president.*

Four

It rained on Tuesday.

As Mom drove us to school, I leaned my head back and watched the wipers smooth out the raindrops on the windshield. Streetlights and brake lights sparkled for a second like Christmas lights and then reappeared as bright points of light after the blades went by. Monica and Mom were talking about a sweater sale at Penney's. Josh was busy with his portable Super Mario game. The rain, the rhythm of the wipers, and the scenery going by helped me get lost in my thoughts about the day.

Rain and I did not get along well. I would get soaked transferring from the car to the wheelchair. My hands and shirt sleeves would get dirty from wheeling the wet hand rims on my chair. And whatever water didn't get on me would be left as a trail behind me, telling everyone that "the girl in the wheelchair" had been by.

And today's rain was even more discouraging than usual. I had to arrive early at my second period literature class to meet Mr. Dempsey. Ever since he had approached me yesterday, I had been trying to wipe away like a wiper blade any thoughts of what he might want. But the thought kept coming back to worry me like raindrops dampening my spirits.

I had to accept the fact that rain, as well as teachers and F's on English papers, were all a part of life. But that didn't make me feel better. It just made me wish for the whole thing to be over.

Mom pulled up to the school curb, hurried to unfold my chair, and then threw a raincoat over my head as together we transferred me into my chair. I waved good-bye and raced between raindrops to get inside. With my raincoat still on, I veered right and left, heading down the hallway to my locker. My wet, bulky raincoat and the crowded hallway made the task of getting into the locker even more frustrating. I grabbed my books and slammed the door shut.

※ ※ ※

Social sciences class had gone over the bell, and I realized there was no way I could be early for Mr. Dempsey.

I zipped out the door, made the corner on one wheel, and headed for literature class. In my attempt not to be late, I accidentally wheeled over a few toes.

Mr. Dempsey was looking through some papers on his desk, but he saw me coming out of the corner of his eye.

"Sorry I couldn't get here any sooner," I apologized.

"That's okay," he replied. "I'm running behind too."

I parked near the blackboard just inside the door.

"Let me get the others started on an assignment, and we can take a couple minutes to talk," he said.

"Sure, no sweat," I said in a voice that betrayed my fear. Mr. Dempsey seemed in too good a mood for such a rainy, gloomy day. Why is it that teachers are always so nice just before they lower the boom and destroy your life?

Mr. Dempsey put away his attendance book and gave the class instructions for the new assignment. Then he said he would be talking with me for the next ten minutes or so.

What a gentleman, I thought, *announcing his intention to murder someone before a large crowd of witnesses!*

He sat down and angled his chair toward me and away from the kids, and then he said something completely unexpected. "Darcy, I wanted you to know I really enjoyed the story you wrote in class yesterday."

Mr. Dempsey saw my shocked expression. "Yes, really. I thought it was excellent. You have a creative way of sharing your thoughts and feelings. And you learned your grammar and spelling well at Willowbrook. But I didn't ask you to come early to tell you that."

I knew it was too good to be true.

"I'd like to invite you to join the Journalism Club. It's responsible for putting out the school newspaper, *The Jordan Jaguar.* There are four teams of reporters, and each team puts out the paper once a month. There's a meeting after school today. Would you be interested?"

My first thought was to say no because for the last twenty-four hours my mind had been filled with thoughts of student government. But then I remembered that Kendra was a reporter, and so was Chip. Doing something with them would be great.

And I did like to write. After all, I had been writing to my Box for the last four years. My Box was like a diary in which I wrote my feelings. In it I also kept ticket stubs, notes from friends, party invitations, and other junk I couldn't throw away.

"Yeah, I'll do it," I said. "I have to check with my mom though to be sure it's okay with her driving schedule. She says she feels more like a cab driver than a mom sometimes."

"That's great, Darcy! I know you'll really enjoy it," said Mr. Dempsey. "You'll be on a reporting team with April Flanagan and Kendra Takahashi. Do you know either of them?"

"Yeah. They're friends of mine," I said. "I've known April a long time, and I just met Kendra yesterday. She and I, and April too, are all running for student government. Sounds like we'll make quite a team."

"Good. You'll fit into the routine in no time. Before you get to work, there are a couple more things I wanted to say. First, I realize I came down rather hard on you yesterday. I apologize. And I'd like you to sit wherever you can wheel to most easily. We can move a couple of desks, and it'll be fine."

I shook my head and smiled. It was nice that he was asking me, a kid, what worked best. "This place by the door will be perfect. It would be easier than making kids move every time I wheel up the aisle."

Mr. Dempsey seemed satisfied, but I could tell he wanted to say more. "I've never had a disabled student in my class before, and I wasn't sure what—well, whether I had to treat you extra hard or let you off a little easier. Your paper helped explain a lot of things to me."

"Like what kinds of things?" I asked, pleased that an adult was treating me like an adult.

Mr. Dempsey explained, "Well, first of all, you're just as bright as, if not brighter than, most kids. I realize your legs don't have anything to do with your brain. But it isn't just that. It was what you wrote at the end of the paper about God and your belief in Him."

I was stunned that a real, live teacher in the middle of this zoo called Jordan Junior High would even mention the word *God* outside of a big argument about evolution in science class. I could tell he was waiting for me to say something.

"Mr. Dempsey, are you, uh, a Christian?" I asked hopefully.

"Yes, I am, Darcy. And I'm glad I've found someone else who loves Jesus." With that, Mr. Dempsey reached out and shook my hand.

Talk about a first-class answer to prayer! *Wait till I tell Mandy.*

As I reached for my backpack, I realized I had goose bumps. I couldn't believe how quickly things had turned around since dragging through the rain-soaked dumps earlier. I opened my book and began the assignment the rest of the class was working on.

Things were definitely looking up.

✳ ✳ ✳

One thing about junior high school—you could never say that one entire day, every moment of the day, was perfect. From one class to the next, the mood could change drastically. My next class, third period phys. ed., was one of those classes that made every day less than perfect.

Having phys. ed. just before lunch is a good deal, because there's more time to get dressed. You don't have to rush to take a test or to be in time for attendance. But despite the extra few minutes, taking showers makes phys. ed. the dread of most junior high kids. I don't have to take showers. I do some aerobic exercises with my arms, but not enough to get me hot and sweaty.

We filed onto the gymnasium floor, and I glanced at the far end where the boys' gym class was gathering. I wasn't distracted for long though because the piercing blast of a whistle cracked the air. Our teacher, Mrs. Crowhurst, was in her drill sergeant mood.

"Get in line, everyone, immediately!" she yelled. We moved quickly, as none of us wanted to cross her. "Basketball tryouts will begin the first week of November, just six weeks away. We'll be working on the fundamentals of basketball in class this month. Some of you may find you do well enough to try out for the team."

She lectured for ten minutes about the rules. Then she split the class into four lines to practice dribbling and passing. I stayed along the wall, watching the fumbled passes and listening to the giggles as patiently as I could. As I watched the other kids have fun, suddenly a thought struck me. I could be part of the basketball team too if I were the manager.

I remembered from the days when Monica was in junior high that the basketball manager handed out towels, collected the balls, kept the first aid stuff, and helped with scoring. I could do those things (I was already handing out towels for gym class) and be a help to the team.

I bravely rolled over to Mrs. Crowhurst, who was surveying the potential recruits and shaking her head. Girls were stumbling, double-dribbling, and whining over broken fingernails. Mrs. Crowhurst was apparently unhappy with what she saw.

"Excuse me, Mrs. Crowhurst, I was wondering—"

"What is it, Darcy?" she snapped. "I'm busy right now. If you need to go to the restroom, just go. You know where it is."

"No. It's not that. I was wondering if . . ." I hesitated. "Never mind. I'll ask later when you're not so busy."

Mrs. Crowhurst turned, mumbled, "Fine," and walked out to the middle of the court. She blew her whistle and announced, "Okay, people, tomorrow we start shooting. Practice dribbling at home the way we did today."

She turned to me as she finished her instructions and yelled across the gym, "Now, Miss DeAngelis, what would you like?"

I was a bit taken aback. I had not intended to ask for the manager's job in front of forty other kids. But I felt put on the spot and didn't want her to think I was afraid. I took a deep breath and confidently called back, "I was wondering if I could try out for manager of the basketball team."

Mrs. Crowhurst frowned impatiently. "Don't be silly, Darcy. Handing out towels in class is one thing; managing a team is quite another. I suggest you find more suitable activities." She turned to the rest of the class and barked, "Hit the showers, ladies!"

Some kids bolted for the door; others stood staring at me and then at Mrs. Crowhurst's back as she went to the phys. ed. office.

I sat in the middle of the court feeling like a complete idiot.

⁂

"I know what you should write about, Darcy." April had that scheming tone of voice, and her eyes were big. "An exposé on certain teachers and why they're so mean. You know, do a report like they do on *Sixty Minutes* or *A Current Affair*. You could be the next Geraldo. You'd have kids coming out of the woodwork with stories—kids like me."

It was 3:30, and Mr. Dempsey had just finished announcing the teams for *The Jordan Jaguar.* I had called Mom from the pay phone in the cafeteria, and she said I could stay after school and join the club. Kendra, April, and I were huddled in one corner of the room.

"Listen, Darce," April said, "our team has to be the best, and a story on mean teachers would be great. You're quiet, and no teacher would suspect you. And it's obvious Mrs. Crowhurst has it in for you." April said "Crowhurst" as if it were a disease. She had also felt the sting of mean teachers. Last week she was ordered to do fifty jumping jacks because she was whispering.

Kendra wasn't so sure of the idea. "Mrs. Crowhurst and a few others are mean, but how would you find out *why* they're mean?"

April interrupted, "You don't really need to learn why. That's not important. We just need an article that talks about how some kids have had to stick their nose in a circle on the blackboard for five minutes. And write about that teacher who still makes kids write 500 times that they won't chew gum or spit paper wads. Honestly, the way we're treated, you'd think we were in elementary school. A really good article about that kind of stuff would blow the lid off the whole thing, and we could relax the rest of the year."

As an eighth grader with a broader perspective, Kendra agreed that there was something wrong with a few of the teachers. "I don't remember it being like this last year except for Mrs. Crowhurst. She has always been tough. Maybe they learned this stuff at a teacher's convention this summer," she said with a laugh.

Whatever the reasons, the idea intrigued me— even if April had thought of it. Maybe there was a conspiracy. Maybe there really were tougher and very secret disciplinary rules being handed down from the Board of Education. Maybe I would expose something really big.

"Maybe it could help me get elected," I said out loud.

April knew I was warming up to the idea. "That's it! Darcy, listen. Remember when I said you ought to run for secretary or v.p. or something safe like that? Forget what I said. If you do this article, I guarantee you'll win."

"I don't know about that, April," Kendra said cautiously. "Darcy could end up getting everyone angry with her—teachers and students—and not get any votes."

We talked in circles for the rest of the meeting. At 4:30 my brother came in to get me. "Mom's waiting, Darcy," Josh said. "Let's go."

"I have to go too," Kendra said. "I'll see you guys tomorrow. Don't make a quick decision about the article, Darcy. I'm not sure it's the right thing to do, but—" she shrugged her shoulders "—it's your decision."

April got her things and walked with me to the front of the building. We raced across the wet pavement to the car. As she opened the front door for me, she leaned over and whispered, "Remember, Darcy, you can make a difference. Go for it."

Five

"Mom, please say yes. Ple-e-ease?" I was pleading over the pay phone in the cafeteria. "Can Mandy stay overnight? They canceled school for the next two days, and I promise we won't stay up."

"I suppose so, if it's all right with Mandy's mother. I can call—hey, wait a minute! Tomorrow's Thursday. What do you mean, they canceled school?"

"Honest, Mom, the principal just announced it. They're closing school because they have to clean out junk from the ceilings. Men in white suits are coming in, and no one is allowed in the building. Isn't it great? Two days off, and it's still early in September! And don't worry, Mom, we're getting a letter from the school that explains it all, so you can trust me."

"I trust you, Darcy. You know that's not—well, never mind. I'll call Mandy's mother, and we'll make the arrangements for rides. Mandy can come over for supper too, I suppose, although I'm not sure what time your father is getting home."

My thoughts wandered as Mom went through her routine of scheduling the world and figuring out how to make everyone happy and organized. She has a way of managing our home as if she were playing chess. Everything she does has to be thought through to the last degree. I have to admit she's usually right about things, but it drives me crazy. I suppose she got to be an expert at planning after my accident. She's the one who worries about every detail—eensy-weensy stuff like whether or not we have a tire pump in the trunk in case I get a flat on my wheelchair or whether or not I can fit through the door of the doctor's office.

I rolled my eyes while Mom talked on until I heard the punch line I was waiting for. "I'm not sure what to do about supper, so I guess we'll stop for pizza on the way home from picking up your sister."

Yes! It worked. You throw a little confusion into any parent's day, and there's always a fifty-fifty chance of getting either pizza or Chinese for supper.

"That's great, Mom! You're super. Bye." I hung up the phone and turned to Mandy, who was waiting for the word. "I'm a genius. You can come for supper and a sleepover and—tah-dah! We're having pizza!"

"All right! Did you tell her what you wanted on it?"

"Oops," I said. "I forgot. But I don't want to call her back. She might change her mind." I laughed. "Not to worry. Mom usually knows what to get. Besides, Monica will be there to put in the order."

School was easy the rest of the day. The teachers were caught off guard by the announcement, so they spent most of the afternoon trying to keep 800 junior high kids from bouncing off the walls. Even kids who were normally obedient ended up getting into trouble.

The last bell rang, and we all, teachers included, rushed for the doors. I lagged behind a little waiting to exit the building in a routine I'd come to enjoy. I had learned how to time the doors when someone went through them so that I could free up my hands and wheel the chair as fast as I could. By the time I got through the second door, I was greased lightning. Then came the wheelchair ramp, which added to my speed. I felt like an Olympic skier bursting through the gates. My mom was waiting in the car at the end of the ramp, with EJ in the backseat.

"Hi, Mom!" I greeted her with a huge smile.

"Well, hello, young lady," she said as she leaned over and opened the car door. "Breaking your back wasn't good enough, I see. You now want to break your neck!"

"Aw, Mom, it's fun. Don't worry, I've got it under control. Say. . ." I paused by the open door. "Can EJ and I walk home from here together? It's such a nice day, and you can take my books in the car."

"I suppose so. I could use the extra time to get to the post office. Be sure to keep a leash on EJ until you get past Pine Boulevard."

"Sure. I'll be safe. C'mon, EJ!" I called. EJ bounded over the front seat and out of the car, greeting me with licks while his back end wagged a mile a minute.

We waved good-bye and took off down the street for some heavy-duty squirrel chasing—after Pine Boulevard, of course. I rolled along the sidewalk under a warm sun, fanned by the breeze swaying oak and maple trees. The leaves, now turning dry and reddish brown, shivered in the wind, letting the sunlight sparkle like diamonds in the sky.

A few of the leaves that had already fallen danced in circles on the sidewalk. As EJ and I approached, the leaves parted onto the grass on both sides of the path, coming back together as we passed by. It looked as if our walk had interrupted their square dance.

The sun, trees, and wind were so refreshing. After a couple of blocks, EJ bolted after a squirrel, and I wheeled more slowly, waiting for him to catch up. It put me in a great mood for thinking.

I really like to think—on purpose, I mean. It's not like daydreaming. I switch into my thinking mode and try to decide things or come up with reasons for why things are the way they are—you know, like Isaac Newton sitting under the apple tree. Sometimes I'll even practice talking with people, as if we were following a script.

It took me only a few seconds to find something to think about. The subject came in a flash, and it caused a strange, burning sensation at the top of my stomach. The feeling moved to my chest and then settled like a hot furnace in my heart. It was like going over the edge of a roller coaster ride—exciting and yet terrifying.

It was Mrs. Crowhurst and the article about mean teachers. Although there was definite terror in the thought of writing such an article, I immediately thought of how the other kids would respect me for writing it. The terror was replaced by the satisfying picture of warm smiles and pats on the back. I pictured myself speaking in front of the whole junior high, interrupted by wild applause and confetti and cheers of thanks from the students. I was presented a community service award and given a written formal apology from the Board of Education. I was then interviewed by the local newspaper and commended not only for my courage, but also for my excellent writing.

I pretended to be humble in the scenes I rehearsed. But after I finished thinking and enjoying all the possibilities, I was left with an empty feeling of embarrassment. I shivered.

Clouds had covered the sun, and the diamonds in the sky had disappeared. There were more leaves on the ground, but they had stopped their playful dancing and were racing down the street. EJ finished his squirrel hunt and walked close beside me again. The wind at our backs eased the walk home, but the gray sky and doubts about my article left me feeling lonely.

※ ※ ※

"Thanks for letting me come over, Mrs. D," Mandy said after we had gathered around the supper table and said grace.

Mom flipped open the lids on the pizza boxes. "You're welcome, Mandy. We enjoy having you. How was everyone's day at school?"

"Fine," said Monica, stuffing her face.

"Boring," said Josh.

"Good," I said.

"It was really great, Mrs. D!" Mandy exclaimed between chews. "Mrs. Fordyce had a baby last month, and today was her first day back. She brought her baby with her at the beginning of the school day and let some of us hold him. Dana Shaw barfed during second period. And Mr. Roth did the coolest lab experiment during science class. He had this machine that makes your hair stand on end when you touch it! And then . . ."

My mom stopped eating her pizza as Mandy went on to describe, in vivid detail and for five minutes, the events of one day at Jordan Junior High. At the end of the speech, Mom stared at me. "Tell me, Darcy, do you go to the same school as Mandy? Or is it that you've only learned to communicate in one-word sentences like 'good' and 'fine'?" Mom rubbed it in with a smile.

"Mother! Mandy and I are in different classes— that's all."

"And nothing happens in your classes? Do they put all the boring kids and teachers in one class and the exciting ones in another? Would you like me to have the principal switch you into Mandy's classes?" Mom was enjoying herself just a little too much.

I threw down my pizza, pretending to be mad. "Mother!"

"Don't sweat it, Darcy." Mandy stopped me. "I'm the same way as you at my house. It has something to do with being around somebody else's mother, I think.

Hey, I bet you haven't told your mom about Journalism Club," she teased, punching my shoulder.

"I have so! And for your information, I also told her about student government," I shot back.

"And phys. ed. class?" Mandy asked, trying to act innocent. She knew she had let the cat out of the bag with that one.

I mumbled no and reached for another piece of pizza, desperately trying to think of some way to change the subject.

Mom looked over at me. "Well?"

"It was nothing," I said. "Could you pass the cheese shaker, Monica?"

"It was something," interrupted Mandy. "You gotta tell her."

"Come on, Darce, out with it," prodded Monica, wiping her hands on her napkin.

"Yeah! What happened?" asked Josh, finally finding something of interest in the conversation.

"What's up, gang?" Dad asked as he came in the back door and threw his coat over a chair. He was home early from his sales meeting, and we all yelled a greeting. As he rolled up his sleeves to wash his hands in the kitchen sink, I was greatly relieved that everyone's attention was off me.

"Here, honey, a slice of pepperoni with extra

cheese just for you." Mom smiled as she tore him off a piece.

Dad took a big bite, licked his fingers, and then said exactly what I was afraid he would say. "Don't let me interrupt. What were you all talking about?"

"Yes, Darcy," my mom said. "Now that Daddy's here, I'm sure he'd like to know what happened to you in physical education class today. Right, honey?"

Dad had taken another bite, so he mumbled something and nodded.

I let out a big sigh and rolled my eyes. "It was nothing, really! I just asked Mrs. Crowhurst if I could try out for manager of the girls' basketball team, and she laughed at me in front of everyone. That's all."

"Did she really laugh at you, Darcy?" Dad asked.

"Well, she didn't hoot and holler, if that's what you mean, but she wasn't very nice about it. All the kids talk about how nasty she is. It's unbelievable. You can hardly talk during her class—and it's phys. ed., for crying out loud."

I felt the anger catching up with me. Mandy was nodding her head in agreement.

"Everything you do or say is some reason to embarrass you or punish you."

When I finished my speech, Mom took a deep breath and launched into what sounded like a mini-lecture. "Well, Darcy DeAngelis, sounds like it's one of those again."

"One of what?" I asked defensively.

"One of those look-for-the-other-point-of-view situations. Maybe you really are causing Mrs. Crowhurst some problems. Or maybe she's going through something you don't know about."

"That's true," Dad said as he tousled my hair. "There's always another side to the story."

"Maybe," I mumbled, a little hurt that my parents seemed pretty quick to take Mrs. Crowhurst's side. There was more I could have said in my defense, but I knew I wouldn't get very far with Mom, and Dad was already busy looking through the pile of mail somebody had put on the buffet.

I threw my pizza crust back into the box and picked up the dirty napkins. Dinner was over, and we cleaned things up without conversation. I think Mandy felt embarrassed, as I did, that our protests about Mrs. Crowhurst sounded like whining.

Dad dumped some junk mail in the trash. Josh took off for his room to work on a model airplane. A horn honked in the driveway, and Monica left for youth group with her ride. Mom broke up some pizza crust into EJ's dish, and Mandy and I loaded a few things into the dishwasher.

"Can we sleep in Dad's study tonight, Mom?" I asked, sweet as an angel. "I can throw a blanket on the couch, and Mandy can sleep on the floor."

"I think it would be all right, but run it by your father. He'll have to give you permission to watch the TV in there. And don't get into the paperwork on his desk. It's a disaster zone already!" Mom warned.

Dad gave the okay, so Mandy and I dragged our pillows and blankets into the study. We agreed it was the best room in the whole house. It didn't look like one of those studies in the movies where there are a million books and leather everywhere. Dad's study had a special feel to it, and it was full of the neatest things— model planes, a jar of gigantic purple paper clips, a bug collection, a big globe, Norman Rockwell prints on the wall, and all the presents we've ever made for him. My dad didn't read a lot. He just liked to collect stuff. Every visit to his study was a new adventure.

Mandy helped me out of my wheelchair and onto the couch. After we'd enjoyed two hours of TV, popcorn, soda, ice cream, and leftover pizza, Mom and Dad came in to say good night, flick off our lights, and take my wheelchair back into my bedroom where it always got parked. After they left, Mandy and I turned the globe on. It lit up the room with a warm glow. The soft light and the special feeling of the room made it easy to talk.

"So, Mandy, is there any guy in your classes that you really like?" I whispered.

"Yeah, but promise you won't tell or I'll—I'll flatten your wheelchair tires!" Mandy said, stuffing my blanket against my mouth. "It's Brad Getzler. Do you know him?"

Immediately Brad's face flashed into my mind. "Uh-huh. He's in my Spanish class. He's really nice and kind of cute, but he doesn't talk much. Have you traded notes or anything—you know, really looked at each other?"

"Of course! He's in my English, social science, and math classes. We sit next to each other in English," she answered in a dreamy tone of voice. "He doesn't talk too much, but he's really smart. Yesterday we worked on the Middle East map together. He's really funny, but you'd never suspect it.

"Anyway, some of the other girls in the class think I should call him sometime after school. They all call up guys. I don't know. It just seems weird or something. I'm not sure if I should." Mandy's voice trailed off.

She was right on one count—things were weird. We never used to talk about boys, but now it had become our favorite pastime. Just as I was about to take a deep breath and give her some advice, she hit me with the question of the hour. "So who do you like, Darcy?"

"I knew you were going to ask me that," I said, glad for the attention but realizing I was on the spot. "I've met some new boys, but I don't know. I think I . . . well, you know . . . I still like Chip."

I said those last four words as though I were saying a line in a romantic movie. I'd known Chip for as long as I could remember. I had a safe, secure feeling knowing that my feelings for him had been growing for a long, long time.

"Good ol' Chip." Mandy sighed.

"Hey, you make it sound like he's a pet dog or something," I said as I threw my pillow at Mandy. "I think Chip is special. He cares a whole lot more than other people. And I think he's really cute. He's getting taller, and his hair doesn't stick out in every direction anymore, and—"

Mandy couldn't contain herself. Using her fingers as imaginary spikes from her head, she made a face and giggled. It made me a little mad, but then I laughed, and she threw my pillow back at me. I grabbed it again and smacked her to make her stop laughing. I was at a disadvantage since I had to stay on the couch, but Mandy was on the floor below me, so I got in the first couple of blows. But once she got her balance, she started whacking me from all sides. In a desperate maneuver, I grabbed one end of the pillow with both hands and let it loose hard against her head.

It would have been a perfect shot, but Mandy ducked at the last minute, and the pillow skimmed across the top of Dad's desk, taking a dozen manila folders with it in the process. We both stopped cold.

"Darcy!" Mandy hissed, a look of horror on her face. "What are we going to do? Your dad's going to kill us!"

I was scared too, but I couldn't stifle my laughter. "Mandy, my dad wouldn't know if his papers were out of order because of us or because of a hurricane! It's always that way. Just pick up the folders and put them on the desk." I pointed to a few on the floor. "He won't notice a thing. I hope."

"He's your dad, Darcy. Don't call me when you get into trouble. Remember, it was your bad aim!"

She finished piling the folders back on the table. The pillow fight and the late hour were slowing us down. I was glad to leave off our talk about Chip and me. Talking about our relationship out loud—even to my best friend—made me feel funny. I leaned down and repositioned my legs and then pulled the blanket up over my shoulders. Socking my pillow into shape, I yawned, enjoying the glow of the globe and the warmth of the blanket.

Mandy had one last question. "Are you really going to write that article—the one about mean teachers?"

"Yeah, I think so." I yawned again.

"Are you really going to list all the teachers who are being nasty and say what they do?"

"I don't know," I said impatiently. I hadn't thought things through like Mandy usually did, and her probing questions bothered me. "It'll be mostly about how kids feel, I think. I'll probably include some names and examples. We learned in Journalism Club that you have to be specific in order for the article to come alive."

"Oh," said Mandy without emotion, obviously not sure she agreed.

We were silent for a while before my thoughts finally caught up with her doubts.

"It's really weird, Mandy. It's like teachers and kids are lined up against each other on opposing sides. I feel like the whole school is a battleground. We get marched around to different rooms at the sound of the bell. We're lined up like British soldiers during the Revolutionary War, and then the teachers shoot at us. They can't miss. We have no place to hide. The trick to surviving is to duck the bullets—bullets made out of words. Some of us get taken prisoner by staying after school. Others go home with red marks on our test papers—like bloodstains," I said dramatically.

I stopped to create one more picture in my mind.

"It's like we don't have any ammunition, Mandy. We get sent into battle with what? Pencils and paper and little desks to protect ourselves. No wonder we do such strange things in junior high. Who can blame us? We're trying to cope with the danger we face every day. They say people under stress will find all kinds of ways to cope." I realized I was already writing the article in my head even as I spoke.

"What we need, Mandy, is a nuclear bomb—a real zinger to help us fight back. And our secret weapon could be an article about what it's like to have mean teachers," I concluded.

It was hard to see Mandy's face in the dim light of the room, so I couldn't tell what she was thinking. She was silent for a long time.

Finally I added, "People need to know our point of view. They need to hear the kids' side of things." I waited for her to say something, anything, to indicate she was in agreement.

At last she spoke. "Just be sure you've thought it through, Darcy. Some teachers have been hard on us, I agree. But I think there's got to be a better way."

Six

"The country bordering Costa Rica is Nicaragua. North of that is Honduras and then Guatemala." Mr. Oliver, our social sciences teacher, droned on in his monotone, reciting the countries of Central America as if it were his grocery list. On this particular Tuesday, I thought the grocery list could have been more interesting.

The only redeeming thing about the class was the opportunity to work on my article. In the back of the room, I was able to make notes on the corner of my notebook without Mr. Oliver seeing me. Mandy's cautions about my plan had faded over the weekend and disappeared altogether with the encouragement I'd been getting from April since then.

I had gotten past the first two points in my outline when the bell rang, moving some of us on to Mr. Dempsey's literature class. I was tempted to keep working on it, but I really liked Mr. Dempsey, and I didn't want him to catch me breaking class rules during his Greek mythology lecture. I tucked away my outline in the back of my Trapper Keeper and gave him my full attention.

As I wheeled to my locker for phys. ed., I had a brainstorm. Why not finish the outline then? My aerobic exercises would be finished quickly, and though I would have preferred to get out onto the court and play basketball with the others, Mrs. Crowhurst would probably have me sitting in the corner as usual. I put all my books away in the locker except for my Trapper Keeper and headed for the gym.

All the kids were dressed and out on the gym floor when Mrs. Crowhurst barked some orders about drills.

"After drills, we're going to have an actual game. You'll split up into the teams assigned last week."

The kids went out on the floor. I volunteered to join one of the teams, knowing I could wheel my chair down the court and dribble at the same time and shoot baskets from my chair too. Mrs. Crowhurst had seen me do all these things. But she said, "Not today, Darcy. You can do extra aerobics and then watch the game."

After some dribbling and passing drills, the game

started. I sat on the sidelines and went through my exercises as quickly as I could. When I was finished, I reached under the cushion of my wheelchair, took out my notebook and pen, and fished for my outline. What I had written so far looked like this:

I. Start the article with a story about Therese having to stay after school for sitting sideways in her chair.

II. Ask a question, "What is going on at Jordan Junior High?"

III. Write about punishments given that are unfair.

IV. Write about how teachers talk to the kids.

V. Write about the amount of homework given.

VI. Conclusion: Something should be done.

I fleshed out the outline a bit more, and when I was finished, I looked it over. It was good stuff. I began making sub-points under the Roman numerals, filling in names of kids I would interview for each story. I made notes of which teachers I would use as examples. I was so lost in my excitement, I didn't hear Mrs. Crowhurst until it was too late.

"Miss DeAngelis, I realize you're not playing, but you are to concentrate on the game. Even if you could have been basketball manager, it's obvious you would not have been a good choice." She walked toward me as she spoke.

Stunned by the sudden attention, I forgot all about

the outline on my lap until she was five feet in front of me. I quickly closed my notebook, but it was too late.

"You know what you're to do with that, don't you?" She pointed to the outline, which was sticking half out of my notebook.

I knew. If you got caught passing a note in Mrs. Crowhurst's class, you had to post it on the bulletin board by the locker rooms for everyone to see. Even though I was paralyzed, I was sure I felt a hole in the pit of my stomach. My face flushed red, then went white. I stared at the floor. My legs, which shook uncontrollably when I was nervous, now jerked violently, as if they wanted to really get up and run. I heard a kid yell out, "Hey, she's been healed!"

"Take the note to the bulletin board and post it," Mrs. Crowhurst snapped.

My legs stopped shaking, and my emotions took over. *How could she do this to me? I don't even get to play basketball, and now she's humiliating me in front of everyone.*

Suddenly sheer panic took the place of humiliation. I realized with horror that I had actually written Mrs. Crowhurst's name under Part III, sub-point A.

As I wheeled by the kids toward the bulletin board, I could hear their whispered comments. "I wonder who it's about." "Boy, Darcy, are you in trouble."

Ordinarily comments like that would embarrass me, but as I stopped in front of the bulletin board, I could only think of what would happen when Mrs. Crowhurst read the outline. The article would be dead in the water. Worse yet, I would get the punishment of my life. Maybe I'd even be suspended.

In Willowbrook Elementary I had never gotten into this kind of trouble. I felt as though my chance at fitting into the junior high scene—let alone at winning the election—was being sucked down the tubes. I would be marked as a delinquent. A rebel. A trouble-maker.

Slowly I reached up and tacked the paper to the board. Because I could only reach the bottom edge, the outline hung far below everything else. It was as if a neon light was placed over it saying, "READ ME!"

With my back turned to everyone, my tears flowed freely. Once in a while it's nice to be in a wheel-chair. I didn't have to worry about going back out onto the court. I didn't even have to turn around and face everyone.

A whistle blew behind me, and I could hear kids going up and down the court. My tears stopped. I turned and made my way back to the corner where Mrs. Crowhurst had directed me to go.

At the other end of the gym the boys were barreling down the court, doing their thing. Every once in a while the girls on our side of the gym missed the ball, and it bounced toward the boys. Then one of the girls would daintily run into no-woman's land to retrieve it.

Stupid game . . . stupid girls. I tried to make myself feel better. I glanced over at the bulletin board and focused my eyes on my outline. It was moving in the breeze as kids ran by. I stared at it, trying to figure out how I was going to keep Mrs. Crowhurst from seeing it. I had to get that piece of paper! Mrs. Crowhurst usually let the offender take her note home after a while, so it wouldn't be stealing for me to take it down. Unfortunately, I was sixty feet away from the outline, and every kid in class would pass the bulletin board before me. And by then there would be a large crowd, making it impossible for me to grab it.

Then it hit me. April! She could help!

I spotted her at mid-court just getting a pass from Megan. She began dribbling toward my end of the court. From the sideline I could see her face. I waved, and we made eye contact. I then motioned frantically for her to come over.

She got the message and passed off to Melissa and then ran over to my side, pretending to tie her shoe.

"What's up, Darce?" she whispered, glancing around for Mrs. Crowhurst.

"You gotta help me. That note on the board isn't a note. It's my outline for the article about the mean teachers."

"You're kidding!"

"No. You have to grab it off the board before the other kids or Mrs. Crowhurst see it! When the bell rings, race over there as fast as you can and take it down. Please."

"No sweat, kiddo. I have it under control," April said confidently as she went back into the game.

No sweat, kiddo. For some reason I didn't like the cocky way she said it, but I had no choice but to trust her. My life was in April's hands.

The game continued for what seemed like forever. The whole time I had to protect the outline with my eyes, hoping no one would wander over to check it out.

The bell rang, and I shot a look at April. She was already on her way.

"Mrs. Crowhurst," I called out quickly, hoping to distract her.

"Yes, Miss DeAngelis?"

"Uh . . . I just wanted to say—" I watched April from a distance. She was clearly ahead of the other kids and would have the outline in her hands soon. "—that

I'm really sorry and that I'll never do something so stupid again."

"Fine. Go get ready for your next class. Pick up any towels you find on the floor before you go," she said flatly.

I didn't mind the thought of picking up wet towels. My distraction had worked. April had the outline in her hand!

April, you're terrific. You saved me.

My thoughts of salvation didn't last long. To my horror I saw that April had other plans for the outline. As the girls headed toward the locker room, April called over a select few and showed it to them! I couldn't believe it.

"How in the world . . . ? What does she . . . ?" I stammered to myself. I couldn't think straight. I was ruined again.

In order to pick up towels, I had to go into the locker room and face the laughter and humiliation. It wasn't supposed to be this way. I was supposed to write and publish the article and get everyone excited and behind me. Now I was sure they would just tell the first teacher they saw what I was up to, and I'd be done for.

I turned the corner into the locker room and heard, "Hey, Darcy!" It was Sylvia Farbman. I prepared for the worst.

☙

"Great article you're writing, girl. It's just what this place needs. I can't stand Crowhurst. She's as mean as—"

"And Oliver. That geek has—"

"Don't forget Simpson!"

Girls chimed in from all over the locker room in hushed enthusiasm, not wanting to get caught by Mrs. Crowhurst, but at the same time wanting to be part of the revolution.

My tense nerves relaxed. I just smiled and said, "Well, we gotta do something. Right, guys?"

"You're just being modest," April said. "Hey, guys, Darcy is running for student government president. She may be in a wheelchair, but, hey, she's cool. I've known her since second grade. She'll make a great president!"

A few "yeahs" of agreement could be heard before Mrs. Crowhurst walked in and interrupted us. "If you ladies want to get dressed before your wedding day, you better move it now!"

As quickly as the crowd had gathered around me, it dispersed, leaving me and my wheelchair in a puddle of shower water and a few scattered towels.

Mrs. Crowhurst walked up to me, folded her arms, and said, "You may pick up the towels, Miss DeAngelis. And be sure to be back tomorrow with a better attitude."

"Yes, ma'am," I said.

The locker room scene was the highlight of my day. I had to admit, April had known what she was doing. I ran into her after leaving the gym.

"I couldn't believe you did that, April. I was ready to kill you."

"Hey, there's one thing I know, Darcy, and that's how to get people to like you. Mandy may be smart, but she's not street-smart. Leave her to the campaign posters and slogans. I'll do the street-talking. With you as president and me as treasurer, we'll have a great time and lots of cool friends."

"Thanks, April. You're a real buddy. I remember when we didn't get along sometimes, but, hey, you just saved my life."

"No sweat, kiddo," said April as she pointed her two fingers at me and shot them like pistols. It was an affectionate sign that she was looking out for me.

❊ ❊ ❊

I was really pumped when I got to lunch. Kids were giving me the thumbs-up and slaps on the back all the way to the food line. Toward the front of the line, I saw Mandy and Chip.

"Hi, guys," I called out. Mandy motioned for me to join them, and Chip made way for me to fit in.

"I want to sit with you guys during lunch. You won't believe what happened in phys. ed. last period! Anyway, Chip, I want you to read my outline for the investigative story I'm writing for the paper. We're not on the same team in Journalism Club, but I'd really like your opinion. Can you look it over?" I asked eagerly.

"Sure. Sounds like it's something big," he said as he gave his lunch money to the cafeteria worker.

"You better believe it. This will be the best thing to hit Jordan Junior High this year. No stupid poems or movie reviews for our paper. This is big time."

When we got to a table and put our trays down, I handed Chip my outline. He munched on his sloppy joe while he read. And read. He didn't say anything or even react with a smile or a raised eyebrow—not a clue! Finally he looked at me with soft eyes. "Have any of the other kids looked this over, Darcy?"

I shrugged my shoulders. "April read it, and a bunch of girls in my phys. ed. class. They really thought it was great. Don't you?"

"I don't know. It seems like, well . . . It just seems like you're getting into something pretty deep," he remarked.

"Well, of course it's deep, Chip. How else can we make this a better school?" I couldn't believe he wasn't excited. My voice began to tighten, and my face got hot.

"Darcy, I think I agree with Chip," Mandy put in. "It seems like you're taking on teachers and not considering their feelings at all. A lot more goes on in school than what happens between a teacher and a kid in a classroom."

I snapped my head to look at Mandy. Now my best friend was against me. But before I could say anything, Chip added, "I don't think it's really a Christian thing to do. If we have a problem, we're supposed to go to the person, not to everyone else. And even if we don't like the teachers, we still have to respect them, don't you think?"

"Respect them? Consider their feelings? I can't believe it. You guys are no help. First you don't support me, and then you turn this into a Sunday school class. You don't get it, do you?" I felt my voice rising, but I continued on. "I'm trying to make things better. You even said so yourself, Mandy—you said that something had to be done. And now you're just chickening out!"

I was steaming. How dare Chip ask if it were something a Christian should do? Of course it was. We Christians had to stand up for what was right, didn't we? He was probably just jealous of the article and the attention I was getting. And maybe—maybe he didn't care about my feelings because Kendra was becoming more important to him!

"You wait, Chip. You'll see!" I shoved the milk car-
ton on my tray and stormed away, nearly wheeling into
a cook and a teacher's aide on my way out.

I didn't want to look back at Chip and Mandy, but
as I left the cafeteria, I saw them out of the corner of
my eye. They were still at the table, looking sadly in
my direction and talking.

I knew I had to write my article. And I was beginning to discover who my real friends were. My choice
was made.

Seven

April, Kendra, and I met in Journalism Club after school Thursday afternoon.

"Can you believe it?" April asked excitedly as she came into the room and gave me a high five. "We're going to turn the whole school upside down with Darcy's article."

"Yeah, I've heard a lot of talk already. Even the kids in eighth grade with me think it's pretty cool. Sounds like you're doing a good job, Darcy," Kendra agreed.

"It's okay so far. What I need are more facts, stories—the kind of stuff you get from interviews and from observations. Got any ideas?"

"For starters you could talk with kids during

lunch in the courtyard. I'll round up a bunch for you," April volunteered.

"I hope you're taking notes, Darcy. The paper comes out next Wednesday. Write down everything that happens to you as well as what you see happening to other kids," added Kendra.

"Good ideas. I think I'll also start moving around quietly during the day. I'll go where teachers hang out to see if I can hear anything. I could sit near the teachers' mailboxes in the office, as if I'm waiting for a pass or something. Then I can sit near the teachers' aides in the lunchroom. Maybe—I know! I can go into Mrs. Crowhurst's office during phys. ed. and check around. I saw on *Prime Time Live* how reporters learn things about people. They even go through their garbage!"

"Yu-u-uck. How could they do that?" April squirmed.

"It's good reporting, that's how!" I said.

Mr. Dempsey had been making his rounds of the room and came up behind us. "So, team, what are you planning for your first issue?"

"Uh, well, April's going to do a movie review. And I've got two kids that have written poems," Kendra answered.

"Yeah, and I was thinking of doing a story about

who really discovered America," I added. I wasn't lying. I really was thinking about it.

Mr. Dempsey scribbled some notes on his clipboard. "Sounds like you're making progress. Do you have an investigative story picked out yet?"

Gulp. We all looked at each other.

"Well . . . uh . . . kind of. We're not sure yet. But it's a secret, and we can't tell you. Journalist's privilege, you know," April stumbled through an explanation.

"Okay," Mr. Dempsey laughed. "Just don't end up in jail like some reporters do, defending their constitutional rights!"

Kendra and I looked at each other. It had occurred to us at exactly the same moment that what we were doing might get us in some trouble. Mr. Dempsey moved on to another table.

"C'mon, you two," April interrupted our thoughts. "This is *our* paper, remember? Mr. Dempsey told us that we could print whatever we wanted as long as it didn't use bad language or hurt someone knowingly and unfairly. And throwing the light on Old 'Crow-worst' isn't unfair. It's the right thing to do!"

"I guess you're right," I said slowly, still remembering what Chip had said. "I just don't want to blow it—that's all."

"It's almost time for my bus," said Kendra. "We

have to finish up here. By the way, do either of you want
to go to the mall with me tomorrow after school? My
mom's driving and can drop us off."

"I wish I could," said April, disappointed. "I've got
cheerleading practice till five. Maybe another day."

"I can go," I said. "I'm sure my mom won't mind."

We finished talking about some of the other arti-
cles that would be in our issue of *The Jordan Jaguar.* As
we talked, I watched Kendra and thought what a neat
person she was. She was not only popular, but she was
incredibly beautiful. She had captured the attention of
even a few seventh grade boys. She had rich, dark hair
and deep brown eyes. She looked mysterious—like one
of those TV ads that show Asian flight attendants serv-
ing coffee and tea on the way to Hong Kong.

I was a little jealous of Kendra's popularity and
looks and the fact that she knew Chip. But my jeal-
ousy faded as I realized she wanted to be friends with
me. She, an eighth grader, had invited me, a disabled
seventh grader, to go shopping with her. Her first invitation to go to the roller skating rink was politeness.
Her second invitation was friendship.

It struck me then that what I had wished for more
than anything this year was coming true. I was "fitting
in." I was normal. I was liked. That thought lingered
with me the rest of the day like a cup of hot chocolate.

✵ ✵ ✵

I spent the next day collecting facts for my article. I was glad that despite my argument with Mandy and Chip, Mandy was still making posters for my campaign. That let me concentrate on what I knew would be my ticket to victory.

In the hall before homeroom, I asked kids questions about their teachers, focusing especially on Mrs. Crowhurst. Lots of kids had already heard about the article I was doing and couldn't wait to volunteer information. It was hard to write it all down, as two or three kids would all talk at once.

By the time second period was over, news had traveled fast. I found several notes stuffed in between the air slats on my locker. It was amazing! I knew my story was a good idea, but I didn't think it would get so big, so fast.

It was during phys. ed. that I decided to take a great risk. As the guys and girls split up and went to opposite ends of the gym floor, I asked Mrs. Crowhurst if I could use the restroom. She nodded, and I headed for the locker room.

I really did have to use the restroom, but that wasn't all. Once inside the locker room, I pursued my primary mission—checking out Mrs. Crowhurst's office to see what I could learn.

The room was rather plain. An old gray desk and a broken armchair stood in the center of the room. There was a small bouquet of wild flowers in a glass vase on the desk. To one side of the desk on the wall was a large set of bookshelves. Half were filled with files, the other half with books about anatomy and sports medicine.

Not much of a story here, I thought. There were no funny posters, no family pictures, no signs of a person who is happy or nice. All the place said about Mrs. Crowhurst was that she was boring.

Boring, in addition to being mean.

Hearing a lot of whistle-blowing in the gym, I felt confident that Mrs. Crowhurst would not return to her office anytime soon. I examined the books closely to see what she put into her brain: *Physical Education: A Creative Approach, Fundamentals of Basketball, Disability Awareness, Coaching—*

Wait a minute! *Disability Awareness!* I couldn't believe it. Why would Mrs. Crowhurst have a book about disabilities? My hand reached for the book but pulled back at the last minute. I noticed it had gotten quiet in the gym. There were no bouncing balls or screaming whistles. I decided against any further spy work and quickly wheeled out of her office and back to the gym.

The excitement of spying was still with me as I rolled onto the court and joined the rest of the class who had gathered in a circle around Mrs. Crowhurst. She was giving a lecture, of sorts.

"You've all been improving this past week. You still need to work on staying with the person you're supposed to guard on defense. Melissa, I know you're an excellent player, but you have to pass the ball more often. All of you will get a chance to practice passing tomorrow. Before you take a shot, your team will have to pass the ball three times, or the score will not count."

"Lisa, you have to stop being afraid of the ball. It's not going to hurt you."

(I knew why Lisa was afraid of the ball. She didn't want to break her fingernails!)

"Megan, you have a good jump shot. Watch out for the extra step you take before shooting. A ref. would call you for traveling."

I watched Mrs. Crowhurst teach the class one person at a time, encouraging each one. Everyone was paying attention. I even thought I saw some kids smile. What could make this person, who really seemed to know a lot about basketball and about teaching, be so boring and so mean? There had to be some reason, some story, that would explain it all.

⁂

School finally ended, and I met Kendra in the circle at the front entrance. The buses had left, and I watched her wave as her mother pulled up in a station wagon. "Mom," Kendra said as she opened the front door, "this is Darcy. Remember, I told you she'd be coming to the mall with us today?"

"Ah, yes, that's fine. I mean, is it all right? I didn't know you were in a wheelchair." Mrs. Takahashi hesitated.

"Don't worry about me," I assured her. "I get around fine on my own."

"Yeah, Mom. You should see her at school."

"Yes, of course. I'm sorry. It's just that I wasn't prepared. Come on in, Darcy. It's nice to meet you. Just let me know what I need to do to help."

As I held onto Kendra's elbow and transferred myself into the backseat, well—you'd have to be me to know how I felt. I didn't feel embarrassed or awkward at Mrs. Takahashi's words. I felt wonderful. Kendra hadn't told her mom I was disabled. It didn't matter to Kendra that I was disabled. It was as if she didn't even notice.

My friend folded my wheelchair and put it into the trunk. After buckling in, we drove to the mall.

"We're gonna shop till we drop!" Kendra announced to the world through her open window, and we all laughed.

"Kendra is a great shopper," Mrs. Takahashi said. "I'd hate to see what she'd do if she had a credit card."

We laughed, poking fun at Kendra, and then talked about our favorite stores in town. When the conversation ran out of stores and clothes, it got quiet. Kendra changed the subject.

"Darcy is doing a really good article for the paper, Mom. It's about the teachers at school, especially Mrs. Crowhurst, the phys. ed. teacher."

"Oh, really? What's the article about, Darcy?" Mrs. Takahashi looked at me in the rearview mirror. "I know Mrs. Crowhurst from P.T.A. She's a wonderful woman."

Kendra and I couldn't believe what we heard. Kendra's mom, friends with the Crow? A wonderful woman?

"She's had a pretty rough time the past seven or eight years, especially last year when she had to take a medical leave," Mrs. Takahashi continued.

"How come, Mom?"

"Well, you girls know about her daughter, don't you?"

"No. What about her daughter?" I asked. I couldn't imagine Mrs. Crowhurst with a child.

"She has a daughter, Jessica, about seven years old, with cerebral palsy. And it's really changed Sharon's, I mean, Mrs. Crowhurst's life. She and her husband got divorced a few years after Jessica was born. The strain of raising and caring for Jessica was too much for them, I think. And, of course, she doesn't have a lot of money, being a teacher. I think Jessica had surgery on her hips last year, and that's why her mom took a medical leave from school."

Kendra and I stared at each other in disbelief.

"In fact," Mrs. Takahashi continued innocently, "her house is just down that street over there. Would you like to stop by and see her? Being at her house would probably give you more information for your article, Darcy."

"No!" Kendra blurted. "I mean . . . we can drive by, Mom. Just don't stop—that's all. We really have to get to the mall."

"No problem. It's your article, Darcy. Is that okay with you?"

I nodded to her as she looked at me in her mirror. I couldn't say anything. I was in shock.

We turned down Park Street. Three houses down on the right-hand side was a small, trim, white clapboard house with a few small maple trees out front. As we drove closer, I saw a little girl in the driveway. She was thin, with soft brown hair and big eyes, and she sat in a motorized wheelchair. She was watching some kids play across the street.

I stared at her as we slowly drove by, my face pressed to the window. I never liked being stared at myself, but I couldn't help staring at her.

Then the little girl saw me and smiled. I was taken back by the warmth that came over her face, but I didn't smile back. I just stared.

After we drove down the street and made a turn toward the mall, I looked over at Kendra. She was expressionless, looking straight ahead. I glanced at the rearview mirror. Mrs. Takahashi smiled at me.

I looked back out the window at the rows of houses, my eyes burning with shame. I held back my tears with one thought: *I can't write that article.* My mind was racing. I wondered if it was too late to stop what I had started.

* * *

The mall was crowded. Even though I was with Kendra, I felt alone. We looked at clothes and shoes. We checked out a sale on plastic heart earrings at Accessories Unlimited. We met up with some of Kendra's friends at the Food Court. But all in all, our shopping trip that afternoon had lost its excitement for me.

As happy as I was to spend time with Kendra—
trying on the styles she suggested, taking a break and
sipping an Orange Julius—we both knew that I was
troubled by what we had learned about Mrs. Crowhurst.

After we dumped our cups, we continued our
stroll through the mall, Kendra pushing my chair to
give my hands a rest. I was quiet.

"Are you thinking about Jessica?" she asked.

"Yeah. It's funny. I thought I knew everything and
then—wham—I got hit between the eyes. I feel so bad
for Mrs. Crowhurst. And for Jessica. Her dad's not
around. And Jessica is more disabled than I am. I know
how hard it is on my mom and dad with me to care
for. I can't imagine what it's like for Mrs. Crowhurst."

Kendra stopped pushing my chair and walked
around in front to face me. "What are you going to do,
Darcy? You don't have much time to decide."

I looked at Kendra, wishing she had an idea or that
she could make the problem go away. All she could do
was stand there with her hands in her pockets and a
hopeful took on her face. We both knew it was a question only I could answer.

People pushed by us.

"I don't know," I said. "I just don't know."

Eight

I spent most of Saturday morning moping around the house. Josh was into his cartoons. Monica had gone roller-skating with her friends from the hockey team. Dad was raking leaves out back with EJ. And Mom was folding towels and getting annoyed with me.

"Why don't you call your friends and do something together?" she asked.

"I don't feel like it," I said, picturing Chip and Mandy and our argument in the cafeteria. I couldn't tell Mom about that. And I definitely didn't feel like telling her about Mrs. Crowhurst.

"Well, then either help me with these towels, or go for a wheel over to Mandy's or something. I've got a lot of cleaning to do. I don't need a sourpuss getting in the way of the vacuum cleaner!"

Folding towels was not my idea of a good time, so I left the house. As I wheeled down the driveway, I had the brilliant idea of going horseback riding by myself. I had money in my pocket, and the stables were only four blocks away.

There were a lot of cars in the parking lot when I arrived. A couple of teenagers were sitting on the tailgate of a station wagon, pulling on their boots. One guy was leading three horses over to the water trough, and another was tethering already saddled horses to the hitching post out front.

I asked the woman in the office for my favorite horse, Poncho.

"I'm sorry, Poncho is already out. But Prince is available. He's a new horse, but I think he'll be all right. If Chuck's around, he can help you."

"Sure," I said confidently.

The woman went down the stable aisle looking for Chuck while I wheeled to the ramp. When I saw her again, she was leading a beautiful black Arabian in my direction. What an incredible horse! Prince was the right name for him. He looked like the kind of horse you would see in a movie—like the *Black Stallion*.

"He's beautiful!" I said. "I've always wanted to ride

a horse like that! Hi, Prince." I wheeled toward him and petted his muzzle.

"Chuck said he'd be here in a minute, but I can help you in the meantime."

Prince shook his head when I scratched his nose. His neck muscles tensed, and I saw the rippling of greens and blues and reds reflected from the sun on his black coat. A black rainbow!

I wheeled up the ramp. Prince flinched a bit when my wheelchair came close to his side, but I was able to transfer quickly with the woman's help. I heard a loud, friendly voice behind me. "Going for a ride by your-self today?"

I turned to see my rescuer. "Hi, Chuck."

"Sure you'll be okay?" Chuck asked.

"Yeah, I think so," I answered. "As long as I don't do anything as stupid as I did the last time I was here!"

"Suit yourself. Just be careful with Prince here. He's a good-looking horse, but he can surprise you."

I slapped Prince lightly with the reins to move forward and must have offended his horse pride. He bolted a few steps forward and then leaned lack. I found myself going backward and downward, my back almost parallel with the ground. I grabbed onto the saddle horn quickly and hung on for dear life. Prince was on his hind legs, kicking at the air with his front hooves.

Next he took off around the inside of the ring, kicking the air with his hind legs every once in a while. It wasn't like a bucking horse ride, but it was just as scary. Every time I pulled on the reins, Prince would sit back on his hind legs again and try to dump me. My straps held my legs tight. Just like my last horse-riding disaster, it was up to me and the saddle horn.

"Chuck! Chuck!" I called, trying not to sound too scared.

Chuck dug his heels into his quarter horse and galloped alongside me, trying to corner and calm my wild animal. Prince didn't like his temper tantrum being interrupted and successfully outmaneuvered the quarter horse several times. Eventually Chuck's strong voice and the calm persistence of the quarter horse quieted Prince until he was corralled in the far corner of the ring.

"Hold on, Darcy. I'll guide him back to the ramp. Then we'll get you another horse. Prince just isn't used to beautiful girls yet."

I nodded weakly. "I'm not sure I want to ride just now. Maybe I'll come back next week with a friend."

Chuck laughed. "I never thought I'd say this to anybody in a wheelchair, but if you're going to be a rider, Darcy, you've got to learn to get right back on after you've been frightened. If you don't, you'll

become shy around horses. Eventually you'll stop riding altogether."

"Really?" I asked.

"Really. C'mon. I'll get you another horse, and
we'll go riding together."

The horse he gave me was a black and white pinto
with a short-cropped mane that made him look like a
little boy. As Chuck lifted me up onto the saddle and
helped strap my legs in, my horse—his name was
Cheyenne—stood quietly with no complaints. Finally
we set out on the trail.

Chuck asked about school and about my friends
and about my being disabled. I told him about the car
hitting me when I was in second grade. "One minute I
was riding my bike; the next minute I was in a hospital
bed staring at a long tube attached to my arm. I knew
things were serious when the doctor scraped a needle
along the bottom of my foot, and I couldn't feel anything.

"It was really tough at first since all the kids—even
my best friends, Mandy, Chip, and April—didn't know
how to relate to me in a wheelchair. The only person
they knew in a wheelchair was April's Great-aunt Ethel.
I looked out of place in something we all thought was
for old people. But by the time I got as good in my
wheelchair as Jeff Gordon is with a race car, I was able
to put everyone at ease."

Chuck laughed at the idea of a wheelchair speed demon.

We wandered through some new trails Chuck had recently blazed and cleared that weren't yet open to the public. I felt privileged to go where no paying rider had ever gone. Since Chuck was still a new friend, I didn't feel free to tell him all my feelings about being disabled, how I had learned that feeling okay about myself was the best way to help others feel okay about me. I would have felt awkward trying to explain how important being able to do things like other kids is to me, how excited I had been when my dad found this camp that taught disabled kids how to ride horses. They called it "The Equine Experience for the Physically Challenged." Dumb title, but it was a lot of fun learning to ride.

And riding horses is one of the things I can do that makes me feel . . . normal. When I get lifted out of my chair and onto the horse, I feel really neat. There's no metal and plastic around me. The creak of the leather and the swaying motion of the, horse as it moves are sensations I don't get on my wheelchair. And I like the way I think I look on the horse—like I'm not disabled.

As we rode along, I was wishing I could go to school on a horse, just so the other kids could see me. Being on a horse made me feel tall. I also liked being in control of something big and powerful. I wished I could ride horses forever.

A cool fall breeze that shook more leaves off the trees interrupted my thoughts, and the sun felt warm on my face. The day was so beautiful and Chuck showed such an interest in what was going on in my life that I went on to tell him all about Mrs. Crowhurst, the article, the election, and Jessica.

"Sounds like you've had a couple of busy weeks since I saw you last. How are you feeling about it all?" he asked as our horses ambled along the path.

"Not so good. Terrible actually. I've hurt people, gotten mad at old friends, and acted like a jerk. I wouldn't mind transferring to another school!" I gave half a laugh.

"Have you thought of how you could make things different now that it's gone this far?"

"Not really. Things seem so out of control. It all happened so fast."

"Like Prince?" Chuck asked.

"Yes—just like Prince. I'm holding on for dear life at school, and I'm not enjoying it very much. I thought I wanted to be popular and have lots of friends. But what I thought I wanted isn't turning out to be a lot of fun."

"Like Prince?" Chuck asked again with a laugh.

"Exactly." I laughed too, thinking about how I had all but drooled over the horse's beauty. "He's beautiful, but he sure was scary. All I could do was hold on. He wouldn't obey me at all."

"Well, sometimes we can't get control of things by ourselves. We need a friend who can help us—someone to say, 'It's okay. Just keep holding on, and I'll lead you.'"

Chuck's words were as helpful now as they were when he was calming Prince. His words made sense. That's what I needed—a friend. A real friend to come along beside me.

❋ ❋ ❋

I went to bed early that night, feeling sore in my shoulders and arms from my ride on Prince. Mom pulled my jeans off and folded my things over the wheelchair in the corner of the bedroom. I settled under the covers, leaned on my elbow, and took out a notepad and pen to write to my Box.

My Box was great for those times when I wanted to think and talk about something with someone but didn't have anyone nearby. I wrote:

Dear Box,

It's been a long time, and I don't know where to start. School hasn't been what I hoped it would be. Some things

*are going well. These days it seems a lot of things aren't. It's
mostly me that's not going well.*

*I did enjoy being with my new friend Kendra yester-
day, but I don't think she really understood how awful I
was feeling. You see, I thought I was the cool one when it
came to understanding what it's like to be disabled. I
thought I was sensitive and understanding. Now I realize
I'm like a lot of other people who judge others too quickly.
I don't like myself for that!*

I wanted to write more, but I put my pen down. I
felt a sudden sadness and loneliness, and writing wasn't
helping me feel any better. I was talking to an empty
box, and it didn't have any advice for me. It wasn't really
listening.

I picked up my pen again.

Dear God,

*It's You I've missed, isn't it? I'm sorry. I'm so sorry. I've
missed You, but I just realized it this minute. I'm in a real
mess, and I feel like maybe You're not so happy with me.
I'm sure I deserve it.*

*I hurt, dear God. I was supposed to be happy, fit in,
make friends, and do things for You—like show kids how
You can make a difference in someone's life. But now I feel
like I've failed You. I've spent the whole time thinking
about just me.*

It's so confusing, Lord. I know You love me, but I don't

know how You could. I've hurt some people I love, like
Mandy and Chip. And I thought badly about people like
Mrs. Crowhurst. I'm sorry.

Will You forgive me?

I put down my pen again and cried into my pillow. The tears flowed swiftly, and I sobbed to catch my
breath. All the fears about fitting in, and all the pride I
had in kids liking me flowed out on my bed and
notepad. The words I had just written burst into blue
snowflakes as the tears hit the fresh ink.

I thought I could cry forever, but the pool of hurt
in my heart eventually dried up. I looked up through
my bedroom window into a hazy half-moon.

"I love You, God," I said out loud. I lay back in bed,
staring at the ceiling, and asked softly, "Now what?"

I didn't expect an answer, but my mind seemed
to switch gears, ready to do some serious thinking. I
chose my first topic without any trouble—the article
about the teachers. I had already decided that I couldn't
go through with it. But my mind searched for something to take its place. Something positive. I thought
hard, but there were no answers. I only concluded that
I had to tell April and Kendra of my decision as soon
as possible.

Next topic: student government. Had I really
thought carefully about my reason for running? I had

to admit I had not. Why was I running? That was the question Mandy had asked.

"If it's not to be liked or to fit in, then why should I run?" I asked myself.

"To make a difference," I responded. Yes, I could make a difference—a difference in our school so that kids and teachers got a fair shake, and no one felt left out. I could run for the right reason and make a difference the right way.

I knew I would have very little chance of winning the election if I didn't write the article. Some kids would think I was chicken. Others would see no reason to vote for me if I couldn't make their lives any easier. But I had one last chance to change people's minds, and that was at the assembly meeting on Tuesday morning. Each candidate was to give a speech, and then the kids would vote during lunch. I would give it my best shot.

As I rehearsed the scene for Tuesday in my mind, I pictured Chip and Mandy in the audience. That reminded me that I had to make things right with them too. I had treated them awfully.

For a moment I was afraid that perhaps they wouldn't want to forgive me or be my friends anymore. The thought vanished as quickly as it came. Mandy and Chip would always be my friends. Only friends would tell me the truth when everyone else wanted to use me instead.

I thought about calling them and was reaching for my wheelchair when I noticed the clock on my night stand. Whoops—10:30! There was no way I could call them right now. Mrs. Ellis would think I was rude, and Chip's folks would think I was one of those girls who calls guys at all times of the day or night.

It was frustrating, but I knew it could wait. They would still be my friends tomorrow.

Nine

I squinted in the direction of my bedroom window. The moon had been replaced by bright sun in the corner of the window, awakening me for Sunday morning. I spent a few seconds adjusting to the light and listening to my brother complain down the hallway about having to wear a white shirt and tie for church.

The house was filled with a warm almond aroma—Dad had the coffeemaker on—and I could hear bacon crackling in the pan. Mom and Monica were talking in the bathroom about Monica's latest hairstyle—or lack of one, according to Mom.

I lay back on my pillow, staring at the ceiling and thinking about the day. Take a quick shower, get dressed, eat breakfast, drive to church, rush to Sunday school.

Then it hit me like a big truck. At Sunday school I'd see Chip and Mandy! I had made promises to God the night before. Making plans in the dark was one thing. Carrying them out in the bright sunshine was quite another.

What will I say? Will they really want to talk with me?

I thought about where I would run into them and whether anyone else would be around.

My mom finished the hair routine with Monica and came into my room. "Good morning, sleepyhead! We leave for church in an hour, and you're behind schedule this morning. Need any help?"

"Ummmm . . . okay," I moaned and yawned at the same time.

We went through my routine quickly. I transferred to a shower chair—a plastic wheelchair with holes in the bottom of the seat for water to drain through— and got showered. The warm stream of water felt great, washing all my fogginess away. I hated to turn it off, it felt so good.

After Mom helped me get dressed, I headed down the hall for breakfast. Josh flopped into his chair and struggled to button his top button with one hand while eating french toast with the other. Monica picked through the plate of bacon, looking for the best pieces. She took a bite of bacon and said, "So, Darcy, I heard last night at the game that you're creating quite a stir at your school."

"Where did you hear that?" I whispered.

"From April's brother John."

"Monica," I said, glancing over at Mom and Dad by the stove, "please don't tell them. Besides, I changed my mind. I'm not going to do the article, and I'm going to try and straighten things out. This has been a bad week, and I don't need any more trouble from you."

"Cool your jets, Darce!" Monica said. "I thought it was interesting that my little sister had turned into a radical on wheels. But I'm glad to hear you're not going through with it. Sounded pretty risky if you ask me."

"I didn't ask you," I said, still annoyed. Then, feeling bad and appreciating the fact that she agreed with my decision, I added softly, "But maybe I should have."

Our family finished breakfast and headed out the door, arriving at church with little time to spare. I hurried to class, nervous about seeing Mandy and Chip and not wanting to run into them somewhere out in the hall with everyone else. My heart was racing. I was within ten feet of the classroom door when I heard Mandy's quiet voice behind me.

"Hi, Darcy."

I wheeled around quickly. In Mandy's eyes I saw the same nervousness and hurt that I was feeling, as well as lots of questions. Questions about me, about us.

I started to cry. "Oh, Mandy, I'm so sorry. I've been thinking about everything—the article, my friends, Mrs. Crowhurst. I was all wrong. And I was really nasty with you and Chip. Will you forgive me?"

Mandy didn't say anything. She ran around to the back of my chair, leaned over, and wrapped her arms around me, hugging me close. Our cheeks were pressed tightly together, and our tears mingled as she too began to cry. We ignored the people walking by in the hall.

"I really felt bad, Darcy," Mandy finally whispered. "Sometimes I thought maybe we were too hard on you, and sometimes I was mad at you. Sometimes I thought you were a jerk. Sometimes I wished I could change everything and make it better. I'm just glad you're back. I missed you."

"Jerk, huh?" I said, and we both laughed.

"Yeah, a little jerk on wheels. But a cute jerk!" Mandy laughed as she straightened up and smoothed the crinkled collar of my shirt.

We headed for the restroom before going into class. On the way I told her about the trip to the mall with Kendra and about driving by Mrs. Crowhurst's. I told her what I had thought and felt when I saw Jessica. I also told her about riding Prince and my ride with Chuck, exaggerating just a little the size of Prince and the handsomeness of Chuck.

In the restroom we splashed our faces and blew our noses. It didn't hide the fact that we had been crying, so we decided to sit at the back of the room. After we found our places, I whispered to Mandy, "Have you seen Chip?"

"Not yet. I think he's—oh, there he is."

He was sitting with his friends on the right side of the room in the back. The teacher had started, and it would be another hour before I could talk with him. In the meantime I watched him and the other guys as the teacher talked.

Is he thinking about me at all? I wondered. *Maybe he isn't. Maybe he doesn't feel about me the way Mandy feels about me. He could be thinking about other stuff like videogames and . . . Kendra.* I thought about the tender way he had warned me that day in the cafeteria, and then I watched him whispering jokes to the guys in Sunday school. *He may give good Sunday school lessons in a cafeteria with his Christian friends, but what is he like with the other guys, riding skateboards and playing basketball?*

My thoughts wandered in and out of the class the rest of the hour. I answered a couple of questions the teacher asked, but afterward I couldn't remember much about the lesson.

We all headed for the door at the same time, creating a giant traffic jam of kids funneling through. Chip was at the opposite end of the funnel, and I thought I might not get to see him. But we bumped together as the two sides of the line got through to the hallway.

"Hi, Chip," I said weakly. "Could I talk to you before the worship service starts?"

"Sure." He wasn't being very talkative.

Bad sign, I thought. It made me nervous. I wondered if my thoughts during Sunday school were accurate. Maybe it was easier to make up with Mandy because we were true friends and because she hadn't changed. Maybe now that we were official junior highers, Chip had changed his mind about being friends with me.

"Can I come, Darcy?" Mandy asked.

"Uh . . . yeah, that would be great," I said, not really sure if it was a good idea. I realized though that it might be good to have a friend along in case it didn't go well with Chip. Judging by our conversation up to that point, I could use all the help I could get.

We slipped into the church library. Mandy sat on one of the kids' tables while Chip stood, nervously moving from one foot to the other. *Waiting to escape,* I thought.

"So how are you doing?" I asked.

"Pretty good," he said.

"That's good. Me too . . . I mean, good now, sort of." I paused to catch my breath. "I thought about what you and Mandy said at school last week. You know, about the article. You guys were right."

I told him what I had told Mandy, leaving out the part about Chuck. I also didn't tell him how much I missed him or about my doubts over his friendship.

A smile grew on Chip's face as I talked, and every once in a while he nodded. When I was done, he said something that shocked me.

"I've missed you, Darcy. I thought maybe we wouldn't be friends anymore. You're really special to me, and I've felt lonely the last couple of days, even when I was with the guys."

The room fell silent, and I glanced at Mandy, who was trying not to grin.

I looked back at Chip, who was staring at his feet. I don't think I would have felt any better at that moment if the doctor had told me I could walk again.

"Really? I've missed you and Mandy too. I just wish I had remembered what kind of friends you are and that you wouldn't give up on me so easily. I might not have gotten into this mess if I had listened to you in the first place."

"Hey, don't be down on yourself too much," Mandy advised. "We all make bad choices sometimes. And a lot of kids were encouraging you. You even had eighth graders thinking you were the coolest thing to hit Jordan in a long time."

That reminded me of Kendra, and I told Mandy all about her. "She's really cool—just ask Chip. She's not stuck up like the others, and she doesn't even notice my disability."

"For an eighth grader, I guess she's okay," Chip said. "But I like hanging around you guys."

I breathed a huge sigh of relief. We continued talking until it was time for the worship service to start. On our way down the hall Mandy asked, "What are you going to say to the others at school? Mrs. Crowhurst, for instance?"

"What do you mean? Why should I talk to Mrs. Crowhurst?"

"Well, aren't you going to talk to her about the article?"

"I hadn't thought about it," I responded. "Do I need to?"

Chip spoke up. "Well, she's bound to have heard about it by now. Only people who have been on Mars the last week don't know about your article. And now that you know about her daughter, it just seems that you could do or say something to make her feel better."

I was puzzled and a little defensive. Why should I have to go as far as talking with Mrs. Crowhurst? Making up with my friends seemed a big enough step.

"Like what should I say?" I asked.

"You'll think of something when the time comes," said Mandy. "You're always coming up with great ideas."

A part of me was ready to lash out at my friends again, but then something seemed to quiet my spirit. "I guess so. Won't that be a picture? The Crip making friends with the Crow!"

"Darcy!" scolded Mandy.

"I know, I know. From this day forward, I promise not to call the Crow 'the Crow'! I mean, Mrs. Crowhurst 'the Crow'!"

We laughed as we entered the worship service, then buttoned our lips as the usher handed us bulletins. His stern look made Mandy and me giggle even more as we went down the aisle. We got into our seats just as the choir marched in.

❋ ❋ ❋

When my alarm clock went off Monday morning, the dread of facing Mrs. Crowhurst was the first thing on my mind. It would be the most difficult thing I had ever done in my life. My thoughts were occupied with nothing else during the entire ride to school.

The woman had hardly said a kind word to me ever, and I was going to confess to something I had not yet actually done. On top of that, I was going to have to find some way to befriend her and her daughter!

My thoughts vanished as Mom turned the corner to school. There in front of the building were a hundred kids or more milling around. What in the world was going on? Lots of the kids were yelling. Some were holding up posters that read: "Darcy for President!" "Down with Unfair Teachers!" "Stop the Mean Machine!"

My mom gave me a questioning glance.

"I don't know, Mom," I said nervously. "This is a surprise to me too."

We pulled up into the circle in front of the crowd. Several kids came over to help as I got out of the car. One took my books, another unfolded the wheelchair, and another pushed me up the ramp in front of the crowd.

I heard shouts of, "Way to go, Darcy! We're behind you!" As I got to the top of the ramp, I saw the reason for the crowd.

April.

"Hi, Darcy!" she yelled. "Isn't this great? These are your voters. You're all set for the election Wednesday. I bet you're a shoo-in by now."

"But why . . . how . . . I mean . . ." I stuttered.

"All it takes is some calling. I told the kids all about your article to expose mean teachers. Most of them had already heard about it. I told them to be here for the rally and to bring posters. You'll notice some 'April for Treasurer' signs too, of course. I think 'Stop the Mean Machine' is the best!" April proudly pointed out over the crowd.

"I see. Well, this is great. I just hope . . ."

"Speech! Speech!" someone yelled.

"Yeah, Darcy, say something!" said another.

I turned to the crowd and scrambled for something to say. "Thank you. Thank you very much. I hope I can do a good job. I'm sure we can all make this school a great place to be."

The kids cheered, picturing the end of cruel teachers and unfair punishments. I knew I had to say something to explain my change in plans. "I know many of you—"

The bell rang, and my audience immediately disbanded. It was as though someone had wired a switch from the school bell to the crowd's brain. April and I were left at the top of the ramp, thanking kids as they hustled by.

"I didn't get a chance to finish, April. I have to tell them about my article and—"

"They already know about the article, Darcy. Remember, I called all of them. They're looking forward to hearing you at assembly tomorrow and then seeing your article before the elections. Our paper comes out tomorrow afternoon, right? I can't wait to read the finished piece."

"Yes, but I have to tell you about—"

April was already moving away. "Tell me when we get to Journalism Club with Kendra. Gotta go. See you, Prez!" She took off for class, leaving me alone outside with some trampled posters on the ground.

I tried to avoid the other kids on my way to the locker. I put away some books and headed for my first class. A couple of kids in social sciences gave me pats on the back, and I could only weakly return a half-smile.

I was still feeling depressed after class ended. As I headed for the elevator to get to literature class, I passed kids in the hallway. Several gave me a thumbs-up or a "way to go, Darce"—each encouragement making me more depressed. When I got into the elevator and the doors closed behind me, I felt safe for the first time since I'd arrived at school. My head hurt from thinking about how I was going to solve the mess I was in. Greek mythology was a welcome relief.

"Hello, Darcy. How's the campaign going? Stopped the 'Mean Machine' yet?" Mr. Dempsey asked.

I gasped. "Do you know about that?"

"Why, sure. Everyone saw the signs and your supporters on their way in today. What's it all about?"

"Well . . . it's hard to explain," I said, rubbing my hands together. I tried to tell him what had happened. I confess that I made myself sound more innocent than I was. The pain of finally confessing things to a teacher was overwhelming. I was just glad I hadn't handed in my article this morning in time for the press deadline.

"Aha!" Mr. Dempsey scratched his chin and nodded thoughtfully as I finished my story. "So that's what Mrs. Crowhurst was talking about in the lounge last week."

"What! Mrs. Crowhurst was talking about it?" I panicked.

"Why, yes. She mentioned an outline about teachers on a piece of paper you were working on. She said something about how we teachers can read upside down. She assumed it was for English class or the school paper, so she asked me about it. I told her I

didn't know a thing. Journalist's privilege, I assume?"
Mr. Dempsey looked at me with a thin smile.

"Yes. That was our investigative report, before I
realized that I couldn't go through with it. I suppose
it's back to Christopher Columbus now."

"Oh, I think you can come up with something
more creative than that for our next issue. In the meantime your team can print the paper without an investigative report, considering the circumstances."

"I suppose so," I said. "Right now I've got to
think about facing Mrs. Crowhurst during gym next
period. I have to talk with her about everything. I
think I'll die, but I have to do it." Mr. Dempsey gave
a short laugh. "Why don't you die now and get it over
with? I'll ask an aide to step in here for a few minutes, and I'll go with you right now to see Mrs.
Crowhurst. I don't believe she has a class this period."
He glanced at his watch. "I think this is too important to put off, Darcy."

I gulped. "I hadn't thought of it happening so
soon. But there's no time like the present, I guess."

After the aide arrived, Mr. Dempsey and I made
our way to the gym. I felt my courage rising as we went.
It wasn't like being taken out to be scolded. It was like
walking with a friend, getting moral support.

That was a new thought—a teacher being a friend!

We rounded the corner of the door to the gym. Mrs. Crowhurst was at the far end, pumping up volleyballs.

She looked up to see the two of us come across the floor—I in my wheelchair, Mr. Dempsey in his loafers. A ball bounced out of Mrs. Crowhurst's hand as she laid down the pump and watched us approach.

Ten

"Hi, Sharon," Mr. Dempsey said.

"Hello, Bill," Mrs. Crowhurst replied. "What's up?"

"Darcy wanted to talk with you about something—something you and I discussed in the lounge the other day." Mr. Dempsey put his hand on my shoulder.

I looked up at him to see a reassuring smile. I took a deep breath. "Uh . . . yeah. I wanted to, you know, apologize for something I was going to write." I paused. I wished I could have ended it at that and let Mrs. Crowhurst fill in the rest, since she knew about the article already. But neither of the teachers said anything; they were obviously waiting for me to continue.

"I was going to write about teachers and the way they treat us and the homework we get and, well . . ." I fought to control the nervousness in my voice. "You were the one I was mostly going to write about."

"I don't know what to say, Darcy. I mean, I accept your apology. As a junior high teacher, you learn to ignore a lot of the comments young people make about, you know, personal things. It would be wonderful to be popular and appreciated by all the students, but that doesn't usually happen."

I nodded agreement, beginning to feel a wash of relief. Maybe Mrs. Crowhurst wasn't angry.

She continued, "I admit that I haven't always been a terrific teacher or a terrific person, for that matter. I think I've hurt you." Her voice faltered a little. "It's not an excuse for how I've treated you, but I've been extremely tired and—"

"And you've got Jessica who's disabled and a lot of worries on your mind and a lot of work," I blurted out. I was suddenly overcome with sympathy for Mrs. Crowhurst, and I wanted her to realize that I understood. But as soon as the flood of words escaped me, I was sorry I had opened my mouth.

Mrs. Crowhurst stepped back in surprise. "How did you know about Jessica?"

I felt that I had told some secret, but when I explained how it had all come about, Mrs. Crowhurst seemed to relax a little.

"Jessica is really a pretty girl, Mrs. Crowhurst," I said.

"Do you think so? I suppose you're right." She was rubbing her arms and thinking.

Mr. Dempsey reached over and squeezed her shoulder.

In a strange way my wheelchair was opening a door between my former enemy and me. I said softly, "It's okay, Mrs. Crowhurst. I know what it's like. I know I'm not as disabled as Jessica, and I know you're all alone, but really it's okay. Jessica can do a lot. I know she can." My journalism article was clearly behind us now. In fact, we all seemed to have forgotten it.

"That may be true, Darcy. I'm sure Jessica could do many things. It's just that the school she goes to can only do so much, and I'm just too exhausted after work to do much beyond care for her."

"I have to get back to class," Mr. Dempsey interrupted. "I'll see you later, Sharon. Come back to class if you get done before the bell, Darcy." He walked off, leaving Mrs. Crowhurst and me to continue our conversation.

"I can help!" I said. "I mean, I can be a friend to Jessica. Our wheelchairs are a little different, but I could show her a few of the ropes. I could come around in the afternoon and play, if that's okay with you."

Mrs. Crowhurst was about to say no, but she stopped. She stepped closer and tapped the armrest of my wheelchair, as if to say she realized that this talk with me, another kid in a wheelchair, was no accident.

"Well, Jessica goes to day care from three to about five, when I get home from coaching."

"That's it! I'll help along with the day care center!" I said excitedly.

Mrs. Crowhurst gave me an odd look and then shook her head. "This is all happening a bit fast. I'm not convinced it's a good idea."

"But I'm a kid in a wheelchair, just like Jessica," I insisted. "Mrs. Crowhurst, this is a made-to-order solution. Your house isn't far from mine. And we'd all benefit—you, me, Jessica. . . . Maybe I can even get a couple of my friends involved, if you approve. Please, I can do it. I'll teach her stuff. We'll get books and games and toys. I'll ask my physical therapist if I can borrow some exercise equipment and gadgets. Please?"

She was quiet for a moment, still touching the armrest of my wheelchair and looking at me. "I'll have to think about it, Darcy. I'll talk it over with your mother after you discuss it with her. It would be a big responsibility."

"As April says, 'No sweat, kiddo!'"

Mrs. Crowhurst had a smile of hope on her face.

She even looked as though she liked me. "Darcy, I'm sorry for having been hard on you in class. I guess seeing you reminded me of Jessica. You can do so much more than she can." She was kneeling by my wheelchair, looking me in the eye. "Perhaps that made me angry."

As I smiled at her, I couldn't help but think how dramatically things had changed since the school day had started.

"It's okay," I said. "I understand."

For the first time in two weeks, I really felt good inside—clean and whole. Not even April bothered me when we met at Journalism Club that afternoon.

✳ ✳ ✳

"You what?" April almost screamed in my face. "Are you crazy? How could you? Do you have any idea—" She was so mad she could hardly talk.

I sat way back in my wheelchair, wincing as she went on.

"Darcy, that article was going to win you the election—and me too! I've been riding on your strategy. And now you've gone and blown it all. You haven't got a chance now, Darce. Not a chance!"

"I know, April. But it wasn't right. I couldn't write something that wasn't true. And it would have hurt her.

You should have heard Mrs. Crowhurst talk about Jessica."

"You *talked* with her? You didn't tell her about the article, did you?"

"Yes, I did."

"Darcy DeAngelis, you've lost it! Hey—you didn't tell her about me, did you? Old Crow would kill me!"

"She isn't an old crow, and, no, I didn't tell her about you," I said. Then I mumbled, "Maybe I should have."

Kendra laughed a little. "April, Darcy's right. Winning an election is one thing, but you can't be a jerk just to win."

"I'm not a jerk! Things just need to change around here, and Darcy's turning her back on everyone. She started it. She's got to finish it."

"April, I admit that I did start it," I responded. "And I will finish it—the right way."

April was quiet for a few moments, still searching for an argument. "I still can't believe it. You two can do what you want, but I'm not a part of your election campaign anymore, Darcy. Don't look for help from me tomorrow at the assembly when we give our speeches. You're on your own." She picked up her books and stomped off without saying good-bye.

"Do you think she'll cool down?" Kendra asked.

"Oh, yeah. Her temper is as red as her hair. She'll get over it. Right now we have a paper to worry about—without an investigative report for the front page."

❊ ❊ ❊

Tuesday morning arrived faster than I wanted. The first edition of *The Jordan Jaguar* would soon be rolling off the presses. And my moment to speak had arrived.

"Welcome, Jordan Jaguars, to this year's election assembly," the principal's voice boomed over the sound system in the auditorium. No one paid attention to him. Everyone was talking a mile a minute and looking around for friends. All candidates, including me, had come early and were seated on the stage.

The principal continued as if everyone had heard him. "Today we will be hearing speeches by our candidates. Each one has three minutes to explain why he or she is running for office. You will cast your votes tomorrow—Wednesday—at lunchtime in the cafeteria."

None of the kids had really quieted down, so the principal leaned down into the microphone and said, "I've got one word for those of you who think this assembly is a time to disobey the rules: Quiet! Or you'll be removed immediately."

The talking stopped. Still the principal need not have worried about kids fooling around. There's something about someone your own age giving a speech. You think how terrible it would be to be up there yourself, so you don't give anyone a hard time.

The speeches for each office went smoothly. April got a lot of cheers for her enthusiastic speech about making and spending money.

It was my turn after April. I had made notes on 3 x 5 cards the night before. The edges of the cards were worn from my picking at the corners with sweaty fingers. I wheeled up to the microphone, knowing that the speech I was about to deliver was not what most of the kids were expecting to hear.

"Thank you, fellow students, for being here today." I sounded like a character in an old-time movie. I adjusted the microphone closer to my mouth. "I'm running for president of the student government because. . ."

I looked down into the expectant faces of the kids, who were sitting on the edges of their seats. They couldn't wait for the mean teachers article to come out at lunchtime, and they were ready for a "sneak preview" right now.

". . . I believe this school has a lot to offer. And I think every student should have a chance to enjoy school—no matter what they're like. I will work hard to represent everybody and plan activities that kids in all the grades would enjoy."

The audience sat there like a room full of statues. A few kids gave each other questioning looks. I felt red-hot as I talked about some ideas for activities and school spirit. Then I faced the issue head-on.

"I know many of you were hoping that I'd fight the school administration and the teachers and that I would stop what a few posters called the 'mean machine.' I don't believe that's a good idea, and I don't believe there is any conspiracy among the teachers to come down hard on us kids. I know things are difficult in school, but we students have a lot to do with that."

The "statues" in the audience changed their posture. They were no longer on the edges of their seats. Some guys near the front slouched, rolling their eyes to the ceiling. One pretended he was playing a violin. Another stuck a finger in his open mouth and pretended to vomit. The girls weren't as creative. They just whispered to each other and opened their notebooks or fiddled with their hair and nails. I knew what they were thinking: "This kid's a dud, boring, a loser."

The rustling and moving around in the audience was beginning to get noisy, so I raised my voice a little. "Another thing: I'm not writing the article you heard about. I'm sorry if I've changed my mind, but I think it's the right thing to do."

The time monitor held up the card signaling that my three minutes were up.

"Thank you," I concluded and turned my wheelchair away from the crowd. There was no applause as I went back to my spot, and I even heard what I thought was a boo from some kid in the back.

I didn't want to look at the audience, but I did glance up in time to catch a glimpse of Kendra seated at her place on the stage. She started clapping enthusiastically. That prompted others, including some of the teachers and my other friends, to clap. The rest of the auditorium joined in politely. It was over.

As I entered the cafeteria at lunch period, I felt as if someone had deflated a big balloon. The thumbs-up signs and words of encouragement I had come to know during the last week were gone. I was just another face in a long line of insecure seventh graders waiting for their food.

✳ ✳ ✳

During lunch on Wednesday, we all voted. One of the eighth graders had designed a program to let each kid vote at one of two computer terminals set on a table at the cafeteria exit. When you typed in your name, the ballot with all of the candidates came up on the screen.

Watching from the far side of the cafeteria, I secretly hoped kids would mark my name. Maybe, just maybe, I could squeak out a narrow victory. I pictured kids respecting my decision and voting for me. Maybe I'd even end up with a big victory.

No, Darcy, stop dreaming. You didn't win, I finally said to myself as the victory scene kept getting wilder in my mind.

I was right. I was dreaming. At the end of the day, the tally came in. I got sixty-seven votes. The winner got 431. Not all of the kids voted, and for that I was glad. Getting slaughtered in an election is no fun. I didn't want to see the margin increase any more.

Kendra won easily, as I knew she would. Her speech on school spirit was excellent, and, of course, being so well liked and attractive helped a lot. April surprised everyone by beating her opponent by thirty votes—quite an accomplishment for a seventh grader.

As I entered Journalism Club after school, I took a deep breath and wheeled over to the table where Kendra and April were celebrating their victories. I plopped my books on the table and said as bravely as I could, "Congratulations! You both did a really good job with your speeches. April, you could have run for president!"

"Thanks. I did do a good job, didn't I?" April was halfway between being excited about her win and still being mad at me. "It's too bad you didn't stick with it, Darce. Kids who voted for me would have voted for you. And you'd be my boss right now!"

"Now that would have been exciting!" I said, teasing April and bumping her leg with the foot rest of my wheelchair. "Are you still mad at me?"

"Nah, I guess not. It was your loss. But the next time you get any crazy ideas to run for election, leave me out of it!"

"Finally!" said Kendra. "No one's mad, and Darcy can lead a quiet, peaceful life!"

I imitated an old lady rocking peacefully in a chair and knitting, and we all laughed.

Eleven

After the election my days seemed simpler, more routine. I threw myself into Journalism Club. And Jessica.

Mrs. Crowhurst worked it out with my mother, and I was allowed to visit Jessica three days after school. When I shared what I was doing with Mandy, she got excited and asked to help out too. Even April and Chip decided to get in on the act and come over to Jessica's house whenever they could.

Jessica was eight years old and was able to operate her power wheelchair, which was bright pink with My Little Pony stickers on the frame. She was in second grade at Willowbrook. She spent all day at school and did most of her class work with the help of a teacher's aide. It turned out that Josh knew her from school, but he had never said anything about her to me. Little brothers!

It was really difficult for Jessica to move her arms and legs, and you could barely understand what she was saying.

"Jessica, do you want to play checkers?" I asked one day.

"O . . . I . . . wa . . . oo . . . ay . . . oo-oh," she responded.

"I don't understand. Say it again, okay?"

"I."

"I," I repeated after her.

"Wa."

"Want."

"Oo."

"To."

"Ay."

"Uh, let's see. Did you mean 'say'?"

Jessica shook her head no and repeated, "Ay!"

"Oh-h-h! Play?"

She nodded excitedly. "Oo-oh."

"Who-Oh?"

Jessica could hardly keep from laughing, but she tried to control herself and said very clearly once again, "Oo-oh."

My mind went through all the possible sound

combinations and games I knew. "Oh!" I shouted. "Uno! You want to play Uno!"

She smiled wide, and her eyes lit up.

My physical therapist had given me a board that holds cards for people without the use of their hands. It was about three inches wide and nine inches long with a narrow groove down the middle. Cards could stand up in the groove, and the person could play without holding onto the cards.

I dealt the cards, placing Jessica's in her groove facing her. We played Uno over and over again. Some people would have expected me to let Jessica win every game, but not so. I'm a tough teacher. She only won when she earned it.

Jessica could tell I wasn't letting her win. I think that's why she enjoyed playing with me so much. Someone had finally stopped treating her like a baby.

After the sixth game, the doorbell rang, and April and Mandy came in.

"Hi, Darce. Hi, Jess. How's the card queen sitting on her pink throne doing today?" April asked.

Jessica stretched up tall in her chair and howled a laugh you could hear down the block.

"Hey, I'm a comedienne! Finally someone appreciates me," April boasted.

I winked at Jessica, and she closed both eyes and blinked them back at me.

"Hey, do that again, Jessica," I said. "Wink."

She blinked.

"No!" Mandy encouraged her, winking her own eye. "Wink, not blink."

Jessica blinked again.

"Okay. Here's the physical therapy program for the day, guys," I announced. "Let's teach Jessica to wink. After all, she's going to have to wink at some guy if she's going to get married someday!"

The rest of the afternoon was hilarious. We tried everything. We took Jessica to a mirror. The three of us sat in front of her and winked in unison. April tried to teach her by getting behind her and holding one eye open while Jessica shut the other. Nothing worked.

It was nearly five-thirty when Mrs. Crowhurst returned. Jessica heard the car door and called out, "Ma-a-am. . . my!"

"Mommy's home, right, Jessica?" Mandy asked.

Jessica nodded and smiled.

April tousled Jessica's hair, gave her a hug, and said, "You know, Darcy, Jessica is a lot easier to understand now when she talks. Do you think her speech is improving?"

"I hope so. She goes to a speech therapist at

Willowbrook. Part of it is our getting to know her better. It's pretty hard on Jessica though. In her mind what she's saying sounds perfect. It just doesn't come across that way to other people."

Jessica nodded in agreement, her thin brown hair shaking. Mrs. Crowhurst came in the door, put down her packages, and took off her coat.

"Hi, Mrs. Crowhurst. Welcome home. We were teaching Jessica to wink today. Okay, Jess," I said. "Try a good one for Mom."

Jessica rose up in her chair a few inches, bobbed her head forward, and blinked. Two eyelids squeezed tight. Her face registered her failure.

"That's all right, Jess," April kidded. "You don't need to know how to wink in order to marry a doctor or a lawyer!"

Mrs. Crowhurst gave Jessica a hug and hung up her coat. "Well, girls, I appreciate your coming over. Jessica and I both appreciate it." She sighed. "Say goodbye, Jess."

"Ou-eye."

"Bye." "See ya." April and Mandy started toward the door.

I got to the door behind them, turned my wheelchair around, and readied myself for April and Mandy to ease me and my chair down the single front doorstep. We were almost out the door when I had a brilliant idea.

"Mrs. Crowhurst, do you think we could take Jessica to the stables tomorrow? Mandy and I are going horseback riding, and Jessica could watch."

"Yeah, Mrs. Crowhurst," said Mandy. "It'd be neat for Jessica to see the horses, and she would love seeing somebody like Darcy get out of a wheelchair and up on a horse!"

"Well, I suppose she could. Are you sure it's safe? I mean, she won't be in the way or anything?"

"Not at all. She can watch from the wheelchair ramp," I said.

"How about it, Jess?" Mrs. Crowhurst turned to Jessica.

Jessica gave a hearty yes, her shoulders pumping up and down.

"We'll go right after school," I said.

"See ya, Mrs. Crowhurst," the three of us chimed in as we started for home.

✳ ✳ ✳

The next day after school Mandy and I stopped by to get Jessica. The stables weren't far away, and it was an easy push for me and good exercise for Mandy as she helped Jessica in her power wheelchair up and down a few of the curbs.

Jessica took one look at the horses and squealed. One horse even put his head over the fence and nuzzled her face. She howled and tried her best to pet his nose.

"Say, Darce, do you think we could teach her to ride?" asked Mandy.

"We can't do that. You've got to have special equipment and adult trainers."

"But we could ask Chuck," she suggested. "Maybe we can get her into the handicapped program they've got scheduled this week."

Mandy was a planner. "We can use the money we earn from baby-sitting her. What do you think?"

"I think Mrs. Crowhurst won't go for it," I said.

"Then don't tell her. We'll surprise her after Jessica learns!"

"You're sounding like me, Mandy. That's something I would have thought of," I kidded.

"Then you agree it's a good idea. Let's do it."

We found Chuck over by the feed truck and explained our plan.

He glanced over to where Jessica was sitting on the wheelchair ramp and smiled. "I've seen kids even more disabled than Jessica sit up fine on a horse." But then he took off his cowboy hat, scratched his head, and gave us the bad news. "I'm sorry to disappoint you, but you'll have to get Mrs. Crowhurst to sign a permission slip allowing Jessica to take part in the program. The trainers simply won't let her up on a horse without one. She'll probably need a doctor's slip too."

Mandy and I groaned. Our hopes were dashed.

"But I think I know someone who could convince Mrs. Crowhurst to try it out," Chuck said with a sly grin.

"You do? Who?" I asked.

"Me."

"What do you mean? Do you know Mrs. Crowhurst?" Mandy asked.

"Hey, I was in junior high once too, you know. She was a phys. ed. teacher when I went to Jordan. I remember when Jessica was born."

Our hopes rose again, and we spent the rest of the afternoon clowning around on our horses for Jessica. We pretended that we were in a fancy horse show, and she was the judge. Mandy and I would trot our horses past her so she could observe our fine riding form. Then we pretended to argue in front of Jessica, demanding that she give each of us the blue ribbon. Jessica laughed so hard her little wheelchair shook.

When our rental time on the horses was up, we dismounted, gave our horses to Chuck, and took

Jessica home. On our way home, we explained to Jessica what the handicapped riding class would be like—that they would teach her to hold the reins, mount the horse from the wheelchair ramp, and sit up straight with the straps and supports.

Then I put on my "I'm-in-charge" voice. "But, Jessica, if you want to take this class, you mustn't say anything to your mother about it yet. You've got to let Chuck handle it. Promise?"

Jessica gave a quick nod and her best blink-wink.

※ ※ ※

I don't know what Chuck said to Mrs. Crowhurst, but she agreed to let Jessica try it once. If her daughter liked it and didn't get hurt, she would agree to let her continue.

On the first day of the class, Mandy and I brought Jessica to the stable bright and early. Chuck let us sit by the gate of the show ring so we could have a good view of the adult trainers and the small class of boys and girls in their wheelchairs. Several of the tamest horses were brought into the ring. Each kid in a chair was introduced to a horse. Jessica looked over at Mandy and me and threw back her head in a big grin.

"She's already loving it," Mandy whispered and gave me the elbow.

"Yeah," I agreed, "but the hard part is yet to come."

Teaching Jessica how to get up on a horse was harder than teaching someone like me. I have pretty good balance and the use of my hands. The trainers had to put Jessica on a different kind of saddle that looked like something they would put on an elephant or a camel. She needed two helpers to hold her and lead the horse.

"Won't she get to ride the horse by herself?" I asked the trainer when he came by.

"Maybe," he answered. "We have to see how well Jessica does this week, getting control of her leg muscles to keep herself tight in the saddle. For now she has to get used to the rhythm of the horse. She actually does pretty well with the reins. She's got good concentration on her arms."

"It was from grabbing hold of those Uno cards," I joked as I watched Jessica parade around the arena. I was proud to be a part of Jessica's smile.

After a few more turns, the trainer came over and spoke to Chuck, who was watching with Mandy and me. "I think she's got the hang of it."

Chuck whooped, hollered, and slapped the side of his jeans with his hat. "I'll give Mrs. Crowhurst a call and let her know."

✻ ✻ ✻

Jessica not only enjoyed her first lesson, but she immediately turned into an avid horse lover. She asked me to help her collect horse pictures and made me promise to bring horse books from the school library. The next afternoon we began reading Walter Farley's *The Black Stallion.*

I don't know if it was Jessica's enthusiasm, the trainer's encouragement, or Chuck's persuasiveness that did the trick, but Mrs. Crowhurst gave the go ahead for Jessica to continue.

By the end of the week, we got the good news. Jessica could try going solo on the final day! It would be scary for her, but Mandy and I thought it would probably be even scarier for Mrs. Crowhurst, who would be watching.

Jessica was ready. She had been practicing her turns and leg exercises all week long. You would have thought she was an Olympic athlete the way she prepared.

Saturday Chuck brought Jessica's and my favorite horse over to the ramp where she was waiting. The trainer and Chuck helped Jessica get on Poncho. They positioned her legs and secured the straps. Chuck gently handed her the reins and then patted her leg several times.

"You ready to do it, kid?" he asked.

Jessica looked over at her mom and then grinned at Chuck. With everything set, he and the trainer backed away.

At that, Jessica gave the reins a cowboy jerk, and Poncho began a slow walk around the ring. He was the perfect horse for her. His motions were deliberate and rarely sudden. His gentle moves helped her to concentrate on what to do next. Before we knew it, they had reached the far end of the ring and were on their way toward us.

Cheers rose from our little audience—Chuck, the trainer, Mandy, Mrs. Crowhurst, and me. Jessica was riding off into the sunset, a hero!

"Isn't it great, Mrs. C?" I yelled.

Mrs. Crowhurst didn't answer. She was staring at Jessica, her eyes getting moist. She looked as though her daughter had just won the Nobel prize.

I glowed as I watched her. But then Mrs. Crowhurst's expression changed to one of shock.

Everyone around me was standing and gasping, and I turned quickly to see what had happened. Poncho's saddle was empty. Jessica was on the ground, and the trainers, Chuck included, were running to help her. Apparently Jessica had jerked her arms, which turned Poncho a little more quickly than usual. That caused Jessica to teeter and then slide off the saddle, hitting the ground on her side.

Mrs. Crowhurst rushed to Jessica while Mandy and I watched from behind the fence, too upset to speak. *What have we done? What a stupid idea, to think Jessica could ride a horse. Mrs. Crowhurst will never let her play with us again!*

Mandy must have read my thoughts, because she grabbed my hand and started praying out loud, "Dear God, please don't let anything awful happen to Jessica. Please help everybody to stay calm, especially Darcy. Thank you, God."

I opened my eyes and looked at the crowd gathered around Jessica. To my surprise, I saw Mrs. Crowhurst smiling. They were brushing Jessica off and checking for broken bones. But Jessica was laughing! Mrs. Crowhurst leaned over and gave her daughter a big hug. She seemed proud as a peacock to watch her daughter respond with such courage—and joy!

Mandy turned to me and smiled. "Now *that* was an answer to prayer!"

Everyone came back to their places by the fence, and Chuck helped Jessica back into the saddle. It had not, after all, been such a bad idea for Jessica to learn to ride. We all watched with satisfaction as Jessica completed another turn and stopped at the ramp to be helped down.

"Well, Darcy," Mrs. Crowhurst said, "you've taught Jessica a lot. A couple of months ago she would have cried for an hour after a fall like that. Now she's laughing and wanting to get back on again. I know it's you and the others who taught her that." She reached down and gave me a hug. "Thank you. I hope my daughter grows up to be like you . . . and has friends like you have too."

I smiled shyly and put my arm around Mandy. "Mrs. Crowhurst, I think Jessica is going to make great choices—and great friends too."

The very best of friends, I thought to myself.

Sitting there in the cool October air, I suddenly realized that all those worries I'd had at the beginning of the school year had vanished. I really *had* found out who my best friends were. I not only had old friends like Mandy, April, and Chip, but I had made fantastic new ones like Kendra and Chuck and Jessica and— who would have ever imagined it?—Mrs. Crowhurst.

I tugged at Mandy's sleeve. "Remember that day we prayed in the study room after lunch?"

She nodded.

"You told me to trust God for everything and let Him do it. You were right, you know."

Mandy grinned and gave my shoulder a squeeze. "God is taking care of you, friend."

I looked at her with tears in my eyes. She really was my faithful-forever friend.

We watched while Mrs. Crowhurst lifted Jessica out of her wheelchair and placed her in the front seat of her car. She put Jessica's seat belt on, stowed her wheelchair in the back, and went around to get in on the driver's side.

Jessica looked at me through the car window with her wide, soft eyes, as if she knew what I was thinking. We smiled at each other. We both seemed to know that we too would be faithful-forever friends.

As Mrs. Crowhurst started the car and began to pull away, Jessica stretched, clenched her jaw—and winked.